fish l

In memory of Annie Monypenny

By the same author:

Sibyl's Stories (Pascoe Publishing 1986)

Earlier incarnations of several sections of *fish lips* have been published as short stories in the literary journals *Voices* and *Southerly*, and in the journal of Malaysian Studies, *Kajian Malaysia*. Sections have also been read at the Warana Writers Festival, Brisbane, Queensland; Tilleys Wine Bar in Canberra, ACT; at Varuna, a writers retreat in Katoomba, the Blue Mountains, New South Wales; at the Universiti Sains Malaysia, Pulau Penang, Malaysia; and at The Gallery Cafe in Annandale, Sydney.

*f*ish *l*ips

by

Carolyn van Langenberg

Indra Publishing

Indra Publishing
PO Box 7, Briar Hill, Victoria, 3088, Australia.

© Carolyn van Langenberg, 2001
Typeset in Palatino by Fire Ink Press
Made and Printed in Australia by McPherson's Printing Group.

All rights reserved.
No part of this publication may be reproduced, stored in a retrieval system, or transmitted in any form, or by any means, electronic, mechanical, photocopying, recording or otherwise, without prior written permission of the publisher.

National Library of Australia Cataloguing-in-Publication data:

Van Langenberg, Carolyn.
Fish lips.

ISBN 0 9585805 9 6.

I. Title.

A823.3

Contents

1. fish lips   7

2. Penang, 1970   18

3. sound bites   29

4. and how to see sunshine   43

5. passions   54

6. the house on Jalan Dunn   62

7. a spirit wanders   77

8. a matter of identity   91

9. a nib for a shoe   112

10. with no foothold anywhere,   128

11. at the way station   143

12. aperçu   159

13. all that blue   168

14. history   179

15. underlying the universe   188

Acknowledgements   200

What is more active than the life of the psyche, with its reactions, its multiple impressions, its swells, its dreams, its memories?
– Germaine Dulac, – *Cine magazine*, no 28, Juli 11, 1924: 67-68, as quoted in *To desire differently* by Sandy Flitterman-Lewis.

Do fish have a conscience?
– John Doyle, ABC radio, 1994.

1. *fish lips*

Rose will be remembered.

At formal dinners and at cocktail parties, the intellectuals will hasten to describe her in a language whose blandness will reveal their inability to comprehend her better and her less than good qualities. They will agree that she may have been a victim of her time and place in history, exchange opinions about her femininity, her lack of feminism and censure the past for its inequities, but they will not have the wit to understand how well she knew her chances.

Advertisers, too, will reproduce her, and they will wrap her image round their shell fish. They will press her full lips against the wet glass of their beer bottles. They will copy her dresses which they will shamelessly market as ready-to-wear replicas, and they will believe she was a woman compromised by a greater love of diamonds than of life.

They will not understand the depth of her love, it may be said because they value sex above surrendering to passionate happiness.

But Rose will not flatter these describers of outlines, these students of ephemera, with her contempt. Rather, she will pity their dependence on a single photograph of a face that once belonged to her. For from lips long since nibbled by fish, Rose may sing with the evening tide washing the shores of Penang Island, the Pearl of the Orient.

Rose chose to be elusive.

Socially she was involved in revolution taking as she did Wang Li-tsieng as her lover, crossing the barriers established by the British Colonial Office which approved the early laws of apartheid. Dressed in linen and silk and stepping between the ranked race goers at the Penang Turf Club to steal moments with her man at the E & O, the Eastern and Oriental, she was a young woman to admire. A bravery marked her, not seen as such because she was 'a slip of a thing' with over-reddened lips and she was obsessed by a passion for a particular man whose wealth answered the questions, "Why him? That Chinaman?"

She chose the hats she wore to the races with care. They showed a respect for the local gossips. They were not only worn as an item to protect English skin from the tropical sun, nor merely to complement an outfit, but as an adornment he would recognise from the native persons' section of the grandstand as distinctive, even beautiful on her, yet inconspicuous to everyone other than himself.

Her hats guided his eye, her hats diverted him, binoculars apparently trained on a galloping horse on which he may have gambled a large sum of money.

Imagine those afternoons at the Penang Turf Club! She would arrive dressed in pale lemon linen or a fine sprigged voile edged with lace, a dress fastidiously cut to exaggerate her hips. A large straw hat or a small one with a fine silk veil tipping the point of her nose, her cream gloved hand clutching a cream bag, she was Rose. Altogether the picture she was settled easily among the other women who gathered in the members' section to watch the horses being led to their cages.

These women moved languorously, carefully drawing their skirts with gloved hands to the backs of their thighs, gracefully sitting with their knees pressed together, chatting, exchanging exclamatory remarks behind gloved fingers feathering air near lips greased red.

Such a gesture may have been a signal to Li-tsieng. She may have laid a finger against her veiled cheek, or a shade of five extended the brim of her hat. Whichever, at a certain moment, Rose smiled slightly then edged past the prim knees of the other women to the exit.

Gestures and signals guaranteed to fascinate are not captured by photographers, but a clever one can suggest the style of the person by seeing the length of an eye in the lens, the weight of eyelids, the corners of lips when others want those lips to pout and those eyes to act sultry. Rose in her daily life was not cinematic although she may have informed the cinema thirty years after her death. She was a quick young woman hurrying towards Brook Road. She hailed a rickshaw. "Here! Boy!" A quiet voice, neither shrill nor broad, colonial nevertheless. "To the E & O!" She was practised at giving orders.

The E & O. It was a hotel built along Farquhar Street in Georgetown. Its ambience added to her charm.

A bellboy in Li-tsieng's pay arranged for her to slip through a side entrance of the hotel. Li-tsieng walked through the foyer, his family's wealth an assurance that he should not be questioned by a raised eyebrow or flabby lipped prejudice. For all one knows, the hotel staff understood they should be discreet to protect the many reputations involved, not least the hotel's itself.

Both Li-tsieng and Rose were not quite twenty-one when they began their affair.

When the rumours circulated, she was readily labelled 'a saucy wench', 'a naughty miss', and most certainly some of the women described her to their daughters as 'a disgrace to her family!' Li-tsieng became known, on the strength of this one affair, as a 'ladies' man'. Before he was killed, the Europeans despised him as 'an Oriental with a sinful lust for our women', and respected him for his family's position within the Chinese business community of Georgetown. In truth, when he met Rose, he had a wife, a girl chosen for him on the day of her birth. Rose was his paramour. He loved her as if she was his only friend — according to one interpretation of their lives, which presumed the better female part for the European woman in a triangle of colonial intrigue.

In a deep room, the sound of sea heard lapping the wall of

the esplanade, Rose and Li-tsieng held each other's gaze, both enraptured by the game of love, narcissistically loving and symbiotically swaying in each other's sense of drama. He twirled a silver knobbed cane in one gloved hand and held the brim of his top hat between two fingers of the other gloved hand. She walked round a rattan table. Under the ceiling fan, she peeled off her gloves and lowered her hat. A vase of hibiscus shuddered slightly.

Li-tsieng saw the light on her pale hair. He touched its fineness, his fingers amazed by its silkiness. She unbuttoned her dress. The straps of her Swiss cotton camisole slipped, and he caressed her shoulders with his lips, and she saw his face when she stepped out of her petticoat and unclipped her suspenders and slid her stockings down her legs, but she did not slip off her french knickers. Rose backstepped to the double bed. In love making, too, she liked to seem elusive.

Pinched between the grubby fingers of a research student leafing through old documents that had miraculously survived the Second World War, Rose is an evocation of tropical indolence.

Gillian Hindmarsh, her manner efficient if not brusque, puts a photograph of a young woman aside and assiduously spends an afternoon reading and taking notes about the buildings of Penang. She's writing a history about Malaysian architecture, assessing the colonial and the Saracen and the Chinese influences on the design of modern public buildings. The documents Gillian searches through are interleaved with newspaper clippings and building applications, the appended plans decipherable despite the silverfish tracks etched into draftsman's paper.

When she pauses to stretch her back and straighten her shoulders, massaging a small pain felt at the base of her neck, her gaze falls on the photograph. Gillian notes a slipper satin dress and assigns the soft faced young woman to an era when indulgence was a way of life for the European elite. Ideologically she knows the errors of the period when exploitation was a political persuasion few questioned and those who did were executed or locked away or despatched to insect-ridden islands dotted throughout the Straits of Malacca and the Andaman Sea.

Gillian lifts the photograph and examines it closely. The young woman looks over one shoulder at the viewer, her mouth open so one tooth sparkles. The dress, its spaghetti straps criss-crossing her back, looks dangerously insecure. Her short-cropped hair is crimped into waves pressed around her forehead. Not a remarkable photograph of a woman who could afford to wear the dress to match the hairstyle a designer in Paris or London decreed was correct.

Gillian slips the photograph into her bag, a souvenir of her researching in the dusty offices of the Dewan Sri Penang. It's so like many photographs of the period she's looked at she fails to see the significance in the way the parted lips rise up a little on one side and the corners of the eyes lengthen towards the eye of the lens. For when this portrait was taken Rose was in love with her own voluptuousness.

If there had been no war, she may have become a tedious woman boasting in her old age about her supremacy over other women in the game of love. Li-tsieng may have become one among many, 'a significant beginning'. She may have told stories about Li-tsieng remembering her birthday every year until he died, and more fantastic fictions to prove her charm greater than that of other women. If Rose was a victim of her time and place in history, it was in a way which made her extraordinary rather than pitiable. For when these two were twenty-one, the Japanese bombed and cycled their way down the peninsula, blasting forever the opulence of an Empire.

Li-Tsieng and Rose chose to die.

Stories circulate among the fishermen who ply the waters around Penang Island and among the Malay *kampong* dwellers. They tell of a ghostly music that wafts through the night of the anniversary of the bombing of Georgetown.

Li-tsieng, his unknown face gazing on Rose when the portrait was photographed, left no image for his family to place in front of a jar of ashes. Unsettled by the quality of his faithlessness, his wife did not mourn his death. His family accepted tacitly that he had placed rash love before familial duty. They allowed his soul to pass without ceremony from this world where it should reincarnate as a dog, punishment justly deserved for his feckless behaviour.

Only his mother mourned him. She kept in a silk-covered book the portrait of an elegant young man dressed in a pinstriped suit, a yellow rosebud pinned to his buttonhole. A top hat and a walking cane overlapped his gloved hands. Before she died, the grandmother showed it to the son her son had not known his wife carried within her to Chile. Wang Shi-zheng went back to Penang during the late years of the 1950s to assist several uncles rebuild and expand the Wang family investments.

Gillian, researching her PhD in 1982, knows none of these things.

She packs away her notebooks and runs her hands through her hair. Dust roughens the back of her throat and scratches her eyes. It coats her fingertips and makes her sneeze.

Gillian slips out of the bunker where the library stores its archives. She's fully satisfied with her investigations into the size and number of plans for elaborate private dwellings none of which, she believes, could ever have been built.

A library assistant beams goodwill and she hurries past, afraid her weak smile is insufficient thanks for his help in finding her a good desk and chair and a working lamp. She checks her wristwatch more from habit than need, and busies her lips and nods and vanishes in a tumultuous whirl. She hopes she manages to conceal her impatience with the thought of having to stop for an inconsequential chat with a library assistant.

Gillian hurries to the Cold Store. She orders an ice cream and waits for a new acquaintance, a dredging engineer called

Patrick. The Straits had been silting and the supplies of fish, it was being said, were less than they should be.

Giving a spare thought to the changing pace of life on Penang Island, Gillian writes a few inspirational notes for her thesis. She's drawn into herself, to that place where expectation and how-it-is lean on the new reality of simple paradigms. Her speculation on the historical period 1910-1940, on a delusory way of life, increased in her a sense of bitter longing for a neurotic romance she could not name. Perhaps she has no time to hear it.

In the frame of her real world, a young man with hair swept high like a cockatoo's crest, stares happily above an ice cream melting over his hand. He smiles at the waiter who lifts the soggy cone from the young man's hand to prop it in a plastic holder. The young man stands unsteadily. He sways out of the room. After a few minutes he reappears to drag his chair out and sit again in front of his cone. He lifts it, licks it once, and resumes his contemplation of bliss above the melting ice cream.

The waiter, a lean man resembling the library assistant, whispers to Gillian, "Opium! He is terribly sick! But, if you do not mind, we let him stay."

Gillian is pleasantly gratified by the waiter's admission. And she is shocked by a wave of guilt about her neglect of the library assistant. She notes in her diary that she should buy the library assistant a gift of thanks — and she hates her tawdry desire to pay for his favour rather than share a moment's conviviality with him.

Time, after all, is said and done, is money.

Gillian discusses none of these things with Patrick when he sits sweatily beside her. Patrick Dreher is much younger than she is, twenty-five to her thirty-five. Busily she pushes the photograph of a young woman dressed in an evening gown across the table for him to see. He holds the portrait up to the light to examine it. Gillian breathily informs him of the plans for a strange house, "A mansion, would you believe?

With a submarine dining hall? Don't expect it was ever built," she adds, plucking the sepia portrait from his grey fingers. "Someone dreamt it, I guess. After reading Jules Verne." And she brushes Patrick's fingers with her fingertips and gazes through a fringe of eyelashes at him, and the man with the cockatoo's yellow crest hairstyle smiles ecstatically over his sticky hand.

Overlapped by documentary evidence and underlapped by visual and musical impressions, dreams lose in significance and gain in detail garnered from the movies. Somewhere a camera records the tender ministrations between a couple. Her head turns, her lips move, his hand covers hers, his chin thrusts above an unfinished drink, and we believe we have comprehended the mannerisms of an era like and unlike our own. When the scriptwriter's words are uttered by the actors, and the sound recordist and the cinematographer capture an emblematic image, archetypes solidify, an era is stereotyped.

That day when at work in the library Gillian had struggled to read the faded and eaten characters of an article about a large Chinese family. Accompanying the article was a photograph of several elaborately gowned women and children seated around one elderly man. In turn, they were encircled by a number of young and middle-aged men dressed in European suits suggesting the family belonged to the Chinese elite of Penang. The newspaper was dated December 2, 1941.

She studied the line of seamless faces, the strange silk clothes enveloping small but plump bodies, the dotted black eyes. The photograph of the clan seated around the oldest man and his first wife seemed to be announcing their imminent departure, either from the world or at least from Georgetown. She guessed the family, or clan, had been forewarned to fear the speed and ferocity of the Japanese military descending the longitudes from Manchuria to Australia.

She enjoyed the implications of the photograph, the statement by the clan and the individuals within it, even the elegant young man listed in the caption as Li-tsieng, back row, second from the left, that they were officially gone, not there in Georgetown. They gave themselves the possibility of surfacing on another shore to begin life again. Their lips sealed by the photographer's disclaimer, they may have slipped into the narrow lanes of Georgetown among the more ordinary Chinese whose shops opened onto Jalan Chulia. Would they have stayed to test the winds of fate?

Gillian admits over ice cream that when she sees the old British residences of Georgetown — "The ones deep under trees?" — she hears a silence. "Scratching underneath a saxophone's wailing. You know. The sound of old gramophone records rotating under the weight of the needle arm."

Gillian's spoonful of ice cream follows her memory of the photographed family and her classification of the young woman whose portrait she tucked in her bag. Patrick, lounging, fingers in the change pocket of his jeans, head at an engaging angle, gazes at her far away gazing at photographs, pictures and movies. "Seeing! Watching! Extending memories! Artistically! But how do we really know?"

In the dusty archives, leafing through the newspaper, she had wondered if ordinary Chinese people had been safer in 1942 than the less than ordinary Chinese. Soldiers drawn from the feudal villages of Japan, bombs and incendiary devices cared little for the social distinctions practised rigorously by a colonial society on an island. Gillian had no way of knowing the Wangs were destined to consolidate their subsidiary businesses in Chile.

Nor did she know Li-tsieng sailed back to Penang to die with the young woman whose photographed portrait she found. She had not yet discovered whether the glass dining hall was built. Its fate was unknown to all but those servants who had watched the bomb drop and the water churn as they clapped their hands to their mouths and ears to muffle their cries and to lessen the roar of the water crashing into the dining hall where the young master danced with Rose, his paramour.

When the Japanese declared themselves the government of Penang, those servants for reasons they may have considered irrelevant, were wired together, neck to neck, rowed past the broken glass walls of the dining hall, and they were tossed overboard. They choked and drowned, their wide eyes and squared mouths moaning the silent agony of their murders.

One young Japanese soldier who helped push them to their deaths, dulled from the drudgery of routine killing, long marches and sleepless nights, was startled to see floating under his oar the face of a European woman. Not wanting to attract the derisive wit of his sergeant, he cooled his shock and poked his oar at the face.

Her parted lips seemed to smile. Her short hair fanned a little, her skirt ballooned slowly. She did not bob and roll over from the force of his striking oar. Alarmed by continuous bloodiness, he wanted to expunge the silly smile.

His soul darkened.

He shoved at her face again.

But, like the ghostly woman yearning for her loved one who walked in a storm through the snow-capped mountains near his village, this woman of the tropics smiled and her arms seemed to beckon him into her embrace.

The young soldier, bellowing fear, stood up. His astonished comrades shouted. With a cry to his mother for her forgiveness, he flung his arms skyward and plunged into the water. He struck his head on jagged glass. As he drowned, his blood, streaming like a ribbon, trailed his compatriots to shore.

Only the fish know this.

A saxophone's lowering note fails to interrupt Gillian's fascination with Patrick. She is too distracted by erotic promise to sense a breathing nuzzling her earlobe. Stroking fingertips, she kindles warmth to extinguish her terror of love's pain. Patrick's self-satisfied body unravels. He stands and thrusts his hands into his pockets and looks away. Breathlessly, she bounces at his elbow, adoration freezing the luck to know love.

It is for a fisherman to stare in fright across rippling water at a shimmering whiteness gliding as if dancing to a music haunting the facade of the old E & O. The waters heave. His boat rocks. The space occupied by a wing of decaying rooms blackens, presaging no peace of mind.

The fisherman's body trembles. With foreboding, he begins to pull in his net. His horrid eye sees a woman's arm pitch under restless waters. A body wallows, a skirt undulates. A lipless face smiles at him.

When he chants the words of exorcism above the fisherman, the village *bomoh* denounces a female spirit for enchanting schools of fish to swim with her to another world, and Gillian dreams she greets the woman in the slipper satin gown. She tries to be affable, but the woman looks through her as if she is nothing. Gillian looks over her shoulder to see what might be of greater portent than herself. Black edged with red and a reddening black race towards them. The woman covers her face and sinks. Gillian points her elbow above her head and spans her hands over her face. She wakes up to hear her big scream squeak at the back of her throat. Patrick mumbles, "'T'sokay-okay!" She slides along the length of his back, her cheek rests between his shoulder blades. Again Gillian catches sight of the dreamt one leaning over black wateriness, casting shadowy doubt on the character a young woman may become in a history written for constant replay, a drama presented in fancy dress masquerading as a life that used to be real.

♓

2. Penang, 1970

When Jacqui Dark was a young woman of no more than twenty-two and she stood on the sprung floor of the ballroom in the old E & O, a column of blue light bleached a musician's stand and she saw an historical period lit up for an instant.

This was her first 'overseas adventure'.

This was 1970.

Dust particles span along a sunbeam that ghosted a musician's stand. An old boom microphone bent its corroded head. At the back of the dais, a tattered sky spread its pink satiny breadth. Cardboard stars twinkled a fly-specked light. A crescent moon toppled, its tip pointing into a wide pleat. Nothing else was added to this celestial scenery.

Jacq breasted the stream of dusty light. She may have expected to find a cat and a spoon and a dish with a moon. She may have been catapulted back to Australia where kookaburras laugh at the strange habits of humans. But nothing was released from the dazzle other than a pink sky, a toppling moon, a few desolate, unstarry stars and a battered microphone. No cow mooed to jump a moon. And if she had a vision of herself swinging round a ballroom filled with rustling silk and sweating crooners, waiting for the next dance — 'Let's dance!' — she let it languish under the dust.

In a cool bar, a framed fish swung on the end of a fishing rod. The beery smell of yeast and hops drifted with the coolness down corridors and round empty rooms. Perhaps a saxophone farted, its belched note striking the barman when he slopped a glass of beer on her table.

She was looking around. She was a tourist. And tourists

have a way of halting half-way in an action to hesitate and look behind and to the side. Perhaps a fear of losing time robbed a pico-second from the place they thought they were lost in, their past tense dazzled too brightly by the present-day. Caught askew, tourists do not see the visited place but the one shadowing the back of the imagination where old photographs are dumped or a spectacle, following enlargement for the big screen, swayed.

Were the couple sitting on the other side of the hotel saloon on holiday or on their honeymoon? Jacq stared at them. They looked like the lovers in an old Black & White, *Now, Voyager*, starring Paul Henreid and Bette Davis. Excitedly, she watched when the man lit two cigarettes simultaneously, the way Paul Henreid did, then handed one to the woman. Was she really Bette Davis reliving her moment as Vale? The man steadied his eyes on the woman's. Was he Paul Henreid playing Durrance, … and maybe Jacq was watching his astonishment when an unrecorded throb for his young companion beat his chest.

Jacq shifted her legs. Round the walls fish were flying above oceans. She played with the thought that Bette Davis also performed in a movie called *The Letter* based on a short story by Somerset Maugham, a love story set in the Federated States of Malaya. Bette could be here, a ghostly sort of presence caught in a time warp.

The man gazed smokily at the woman. And Jacq could not keep her eyes off them, accepting the couple as a set piece and, like the photographed fish, part of the decor and not real at all.

Jacq upended the coaster. It was ringed with condensation. She pushed it into her bag and slid the empty beer glass across the table, strode through the foyer and burst onto the street. Blinding light obliterated the shops opposite the hotel. She stumbled and fell, her descent into the tourist's mood for looking at things rapid and almost hurtful.

The smokey-eyed lovers pulled up sharply beside her.

None of them saw the present negotiating the future. They had all three hurried past two businessmen haggling in the breakfast room of the E & O. Their sleeves rolled up above their elbows, the men sipped tea and jabbed fingers at a piece of paper.

Wang Shi-zheng, a man perhaps in his late twenties, planned to build the Merlin Hotel on a garage lot over the road from the E & O. He wanted to build an economically viable Penang out of the somnolence, the Georgetown he flew to when he was in his teens. In the late 1950s, his uncles, BK and Cho, concurred he was a young man with a good talent for business. It was better, they agreed, that he should leave Chile where the family had gone for the duration of the Japanese occupation and where most had chosen to stay.

Notwithstanding the successes of their Chilean enterprises, those uncles, BK and Cho, felt more comfortable where the family wealth originated, in Penang. They salvaged the core of their war-wrecked businesses, and they acquired diverse holdings until the Wangs consolidated their original investments. In the late sixties when Shi-zheng finally joined them after an American education, the Wang empire expanded.

With Shi-zheng behind the operations, the Wangs planned to transform beyond historical recognition the streets his father, the errant Li-tsieng, sped along in a rickshaw before the War, anticipating an afternoon's dalliance at the E & O with Rose. Shi-zheng knew nothing about Li-tsieng, nothing that is, but the unassailable fact that his father had done something wrong.

And Shi-zheng did not connect his father's misdeeds with the unease that set in when the maids gossiped about fishermen gibbering nonsense after they returned with their night catch from the Straits. Bewitched eyes popping, the maids talked of a ghostly woman singing and a saxophone wailing with the evening tide, enchanting fish into unlikely waters. The young man barely noticed his aunts, on hearing of these things from the kitchen staff, were suddenly busy with joss sticks at the family shrine, and generous with their offerings to Guanyin, the Goddess of Mercy. Even so, although he gave little credence to these stories about men terrified by a faltering lament and a face smiling and rolling in their nets, Shi-zheng's skin prickled from the eeriness that chilled the smells of incense wafting through the house. He felt his blood thin painfully. Something inside him drew downwards. But rather than shiver wordlessly and buckle at the knees, he warmed himself up by studying new theories on city planning and the latest methods of accountancy.

True to say, Shi-zheng was not one to sit still. Focussed on the future, he planned how and when to blast the historic dust of sleepy Penang more surely than a Japanese bomb. And several years down the track, in 1983 or 4, the man who was sitting opposite Shi-zheng would contract to have him shot outside one of the Wang family banks. Jacq will read about it in Sydney, a footnote about Malaysian business activities. Sometimes these news items find their way into Australian newspapers, usually under the header *In Brief*.

Flinging one arm over the back of his chair in 1970 and running fingers up and down his glass of tea, Shi-zheng was discussing the demolition of several streets. His future assassin was not in absolute agreement with some of the calculations directly affecting his family's acquisition of properties around one. Leith Street. He was in no doubt he detested the pace driving the expansion of the Wang empire. Shi-zheng, he privately opined, was too American. "Too hasty-lah! Too much West."

Leith Street.
That was the street Jacq saw the smokey-eyed lovers from the hotel walking down.
She followed them.
Elegant arches covered wide footways where turbaned

men, like a thousand Sinbads in infinite renditions of *Arabian Nights*, rolled their legs and pointed their toes to heaven and contorted their arms in ropy tangles. Shyly, Jacq hesitated, afraid she may have slipped with Sinbad the Tailor's thread through an eye in a needle weaving her into a dreamt story she did not understand.

Not bothered by tourists, the owners of these shophouses slowly, slowly, slowly, opened for the afternoon trade. Slowly, slowly, slowly they heaved their plump bodies behind counters hidden under layers of haberdashery, nuts and bolts, toiletries. Slowly, slowly, slowly their stock turned over — garments brittle with age, rusted tins of screws and nails, bottles and bottles of Brylcreme. And Horlicks.

Tamarind and curry leaf mingling with saffron and gingili oil seeped through the smells of old cloth, metal and grease. Perfumed soaps hardened and split in fading paper wrappers. A little dust puffed and spread and settled lightly on goods that had never suffered the indignity of a price markdown or an all-stock-must-go sale.

This was Penang in 1970, at the end of the end of an era. Since the Japanese had withdrawn in 1945, a race riot had been quickly quelled, but nothing else had disturbed its sleepiness. Some of the buildings' chipped paint and pockmarked masonry disguised bullet holes from both periods. Lopsided buildings, sagging on rotting joists, sighed and sighed and sighed.

Wearily, the old town centre repeated the routine of days gone by, wearily it slept. Yet, there was an ambience, there was the languor warming the rows of shophouses — the salty air, the green clarity dominating the hills, and the pearly light shimmering the sea and the sky in the afternoons.

Jacq followed the couple, her smokey-eyed lovers, keeping them at a discreet distance. She was not used to crowds, she felt 'new', an untried traveller who liked to be alone, and she wandered after them into the central markets. She held her breath. Unfamiliar smells she could not name thickened. She stared and stared. At school children, dressed in bright white and navy blue. She ran light fingers over hot pink boiled lollies and sticks of black and brown stuff. "What is it?" she asked. But her voice was too soft. She forced the words to grate over her larynx, "What is it?"

Aah! *Dodol!*

Such a word, one she took a while to grasp.

Wide smiles widened. Soft giggles fascinated an innocence with pellucid charm.

Chinese girls in brief minis bargained for vegetables and peeled back fishes' gills, painted nails daintily pointing above deepening purple. Moon faced office girls swayed with friends languishing in *badju kurung*, the long skirt and long sleeved blouse of the Malays. A Tamil girl, her sloe eyes liquid black, lifted a gold embroidered red silk sari length by the tips of her fingers and, slowly, she swathed it round her thin black arm.

Jacq's head buzzed. She was agog, there was so much colour. If it was a movie snagging her feet, the music groaned, its beat discordant. Was the Tamil girl, for example, dreaming as Sinbad the Tailor did when he dreamt he was Sinbad the Sailor sailing away from his humdrum life for adventures in the fairyland of love and wealth? Will the lion roll its head for MGM, will it growl for that beautiful girl to soar across the big screen in her red silk sari? Or will a giant's hand descend from above to lift her onto a cloud where he will watch her dance, her arms coiling, her eyes flashing laughter?

Jacq was not too sure what a lot of things were about.

She was hot and sweaty. She looked for ice cream. She looked for a chilly airconditioned cafe, and she walked into a place called Cold Store.

She ordered a sundae. When it came, Jacq was surprised how perfectly like an ad it looked. Triangular and colourful wafers poked above the lip of the bowl. A spoon, advancing its handle politely, waited to be lifted, waited to slice into creamy coldness. But the sundae, which was not too generously sprinkled with crushed nuts, was made with Penang ice cream from evaporated milk, not rich dairy cream. Jacq pulled a face, and turned her spoon over in her mouth to lick it clean.

The waiter frowned. He thought her manners were disgusting.

The smokey-eyed lovers paid at the cash register.

Jacq asked for tea. She pulled out a bundle of postcards and wrote out all of them. To her brother, Kel, she described seeing a Bette Davis/Paul Henreid lookalike couple in an old hotel.

That night when she was looking for something to eat, she found the esplanade where hawkers had set up their food stalls. Woks spat sesame seed oil. The air was thick with the smells of fish and chicken frying with dried prawn and chilli paste. Pork smoked over perfumed charcoal. There were soups made from the spare parts of pigs.

Jacq tooled chopsticks through *mie* and an omelette made with local oysters. And the smokey-eyed lovers, picking through fish bones at a nearby table, were questioning an old man about a mansion that was famed for its underwater dining hall.

When startled, Shi-zheng calmed doubts about himself by eating. And the tourists' questions startled him. In Santiago where he spent most of his childhood, if he surprised his aunts by repeating their descriptions of a submarine dining hall, they would severely reprimand him. His Third Grandma, kinder than the others, gave him an old book by Jules Verne about the future when people would live under the sea. She said his great grandfather liked reading Jules Verne's stories and he got the idea to build a submarine dining hall from this one because his favourite food was fish and when he ate it, he liked to see the fish swim around him.

Shi-zheng had no patience for fabulisms. An underwater

dining hall was for him an ostentatious display of wealth that made no wealth. But he was made uneasy when he heard questions about that dining hall. There he was, sitting at his favourite stall slurping his favourite food, pig liver soup. It did not taste too good when it was cold. But with chopsticks and spoon pointing skyward, he peered over his shoulder at the freckled mauvey-white couple standing in front of an old man with their questions. Without any expression, he fixed on them a long gaze.

The old man raised his wizened face and narrowed his eyes as if he focussed them down a tube to recollections of another lifetime. Shi-zheng watched him shake his head slowly, and he heard him say, "Maybe ... Japanese bomb."

When the inquiring couple who looked like out-of-date movie stars heard this, they seemed to crow sadly.

Shi-zheng followed their gaze out to sea.

Jacq shovelled *mie*. The sound of a wash thudded the wall of the esplanade, mixing with a saxophone's long note that may have wound round a pale moon. Jacq, looking up, thought she saw a young woman spinning in a fine satin gown on a moonbeam, ghostly hands spread, ghostly fingers speaking an alphabet. She paused, allowing the moment to subside, and then she continued eating her *mie*.

But her sleep was disturbed.

Throughout the night, fish lips fish-kissed, and fish tails flicked through dreams, and fish stories turned into anglers' pictures on big and small screens. They swam around and around, around and around, until the world dizzied and tipped awry. Challenging the light spooling between weeds, fish back-flipped and side-swiped and darted straight down the line until dawn.

In the morning light, Jacq, exhausted by her dreams of fishy manoeuvrings, watched a gecko dart across the ceiling smack into a moth. With two muscular convulsions of its transparent little body, the gecko ate the moth.

What dawn this?

Outside a grocery shop, Wang Shi-zheng parked his car. The shop awnings offered no shade to protect pedestrians and parked cars from the mid-morning heat.

He walked down the broken footpath between boxes of day-old chickens, bags of rice and crazy stacks of tinned goods — cooking oil, powdered milk, kerosene — to a coffee shop that was in reality an unprepossessing lean-to. He wore a beige shirt over fawn trousers. His black shining hair was slicked, smoothed flat against his brown skull. He seemed to concentrate on the rubble underfoot. If the waiter had not shouted abuse at a tourist, the Bette Davis/Paul Henreid lookalikes who were sipping cold drinks through straws, may have been alerted to an assignation history imposed on the future when Wang Shi-zheng shook hands with his partner in the business of razing the jungle from Penang's hills.

The two men turned into the interior of the coffee shop. They talked over plates of oily noodles about the future growth in the tourist industry and how the population growth would mean a greater demand for housing. Shi-zheng did not discuss his obsession, a new communications technology. His experience of the future instructed his imagination to know his dream, moving money within seconds, was a probability.

Sometimes he sat, noodles trailing off his upraised chopsticks, happily mesmerised by money whizzing around the globe. If his colleague did not interrupt his streaming consciousness, if he did not continue to refine a negotiated detail or two, a ghostly young man embracing a woman whose pale silken hair shimmered as if under restless water would waver across Shi-zheng's pecuniary vision. When that happened, he looked up, blinking. He would shudder to lose a nightdream under the hard light of day. He would force himself to concentrate on a new arrangement of figures he wanted in fact to see balanced stylishly in his ledgers.

In 1970, the enterprising Shi-zheng was interested in tourism, not tourists. He did not meet tourists, although he saw them. He saw Jacqueline Dark. And the couple who looked cinematically familiar.

Jacq was the one the waiter, a bow-legged old man dressed in baggy short pants, shouted at. When he slapped a drink in front of her, the liquid splashed up. She grated her chair backwards over cement then, with the slowness of the dejected, she took a crumpled paper tissue and wiped sticky stuff off her arms.

Shi-zheng sat back in his chair. A journalist, a Malay he knew by sight only, rebuked the waiter, and pulled out a chair for the pale woman. She smiled in a wan sort of way and, as if time dropped its speed, she slowly swam over tables and round chairs, her hair lifting and flowing and falling in a wide slow circle round her face, her bag hovering for crazed minutes above her shoulders, and she sank and sank and sank. Shi-zheng, observing the Malay's good-natured attentiveness, listened for what he might hear. The woman was baffling. Her replies to ordinary inquiries about where are you staying?, where have you been? and what have you seen? were almost dismissive.

Q : Why travel alone?

A : When you travel alone, you have more freedom.

A : Alone, you're free to see and do as you please.

A : Because I value my freedom. Freedom to go to bed ..., write letters to my brother ..., freedom not to be looked at all the time.

Swimming into the journalist's gaze, Jacqueline surprised herself. A voice other than her own said she was planning to stay in Penang to teach English. "I want to have the freedom to look deep into liquid eyes. On my own terms. Whenever the opportunity should arise."

The journalist lowered his eyelids. He concealed how he

may have read in magazines and newspapers, and witnessed at the cinema, that women's frankness was admired in Western countries, but he judged her artlessness to be appalling.

⊬

3. sound bites

What defines the way we see the world?

Some say maps do.

Jacqueline Dark liked the flattened maps in atlases. When they were children, Jacq and her brother, Kel, liked the way the flattened world peaked across the tops of the pages, the way the latitudes and longitudes curved.

They lived in a farmhouse overlooking a swampy flat and midway up a beautifully timbered hill. At their kitchen table, Kel and Jacq pored over pages of maps, their fingers tracing journeys they planned to take. Crammed together in cranky tubs, they tumbled through a black hole in time near a hairy man snarling divinely beside his upheld trident. Round his mouth a beard frothed into foaming waves. His hair tossed and flowed into the seaspray. Their journeys, pitched forward on Poseidon's trident, which defied the curvilinear latitudes and longitudes, transported them into legendary realms.

Globes were never so much fun. They spun the piratical Jacq and Kel away from dramatised stories about dipping over the equator where Poseidon, the giant bunyip guarding the equator, hissed through green teeth and bellowed.

Eye patches in place, swords poked in their belts, they sailed across the painted pages of the atlas, away from the kitchen table where the earth flattened, out of the mapped world, out of the beautiful and bitter valley where they lived into a dazzling bright place. They put to sword a dozen foe. They battled little people Jacq insisted were called Lilliputians, and they gave water to a princess who was dying of thirst. When the sun tipped and shadows tongued the round of a hill, their hulk tipped up its forrard and the flag flew. Jacq and Kel sailed above a green sward. They beached their tub under a silky oak tree, brandished their swords beside a blackbean tree, and marched up wooden steps onto a wooden verandah.

A distant siren screamed.

A woman howled.

In the early years of the 1960s, no one described sad-faced girls as anorexic. No one. Not teachers working the classrooms of country town high schools, and emphatically not the farming families Jacq Dark and her cousins, Gillian and Fi Hindmarsh, belonged to. Jacq seemed to be withdrawn, but the teachers' knowledge of sporting rules far exceeded their ability to tolerate eccentricities.

Gillian remembered her cousin as 'the boys' bad joke'. Every morning she climbed up the old school bus steps to the disharmonic jingle, *Whack Oh Jacqui Darrr'!! Stick This Up Your Flat And Skinny Arrrrrrrr!!!!!!!*

In the distance, a siren screamed.

A woman howled.

Kel's apprehensive eyes glazed over to see nothing.

The timbers of their house shivered, a nervousness twisting from its stumps up into its ceiling where beams creaked in dismay. Fingers to silenced lips, the children slipped into the kitchen where they saw pieces of shattered crockery. Something had been smashed against the window frame.

Jacq rattled a cake tin.

Kel knew their mother welcomed their return from the places not painted on the mapped world. But this day was not the same as other times. It was like a darker time he wanted to forget.

A gust of air whooshed around the house and frightened them. A breathy space a spirit might fill wavered. "It's alright," Jacq whispered to Kel. "It's alright. Pirates are meant to be superstitious."

Kel and Jacq huddled together on the wide verandah. Jacq told Kel the land they lived in sometimes emptied of its mothers. They tried to spread out their atlas and study the maps, the rises and the peaks at the tops of the pages. Stabbing their fingers at islands they wanted to see together, they made a wish to fall down the longitudes onto Poseidon's trident. But when pink lights chased old afternoon gold around the valley and evening dampness stung their bare legs, they curled their arms around each other and quietly listened to the frogs croaking, the gnats hissing, the crickets whirruping down at the creek below their house.

Nothing moved in the valley. No cars zoomed along the bitumen road. The cows were not grazing where the farms were too boggy. Deep green rainforest trees sank down the banks of the widening river. A voice abusing pigs whipcracked, and an echoing of sounds spiralled around and around and around, enclosing the valley and all its living forms within a forbiddingly hermetic seal.

Jacq looked over her shoulder to peer through a doorway into the house. She hoped to hear words. But only the sounds of insects hissed into the furniture.

Jacq clung to the verandah rails and pressed her forehead between them. Kel swung his legs over the edge of the bare boards. They squashed their pale faces between the white wooden rails, their eyes hunting the darkness for their father's green Vauxhall to bump over the tussocks as it nosed up the rough drive. Jacq and Kel waited to see his tired face, to hear him say, "What's it to be? Vegemite and toast? I'm not much good at chops and things."

The house, slanting down at an odd angle, immured the family's confusion.

When she was a university student, Jacqui Dark hoped to find sympathetic listeners to her bent analyses of the squelchy mess of her childhood. But she was met with too much incomprehension. In the end, she chose to retreat to her sunless flat decorated with the acquisitions of the restless traveller, preferring to answer questions about her life with a discretionary and enigmatic smile.

She came from a district where women were known to bay the moon to stifle the silence of a land robbed of its rainforest. And when their wild cries subsided with the dawnlight, the screaming siren of an ambulance racing them to a Brisbane psychiatrist's rooms filled the valleys. The men looked at the ground, fearful one among their family of women — a sister, a wife, a mother — may be the next one to snap. The graveyard emptiness of the valleys that had been cleared of all the life that lived in trees, squirmed under bushes and spun nests in grasses capsized into women's enraged chattering. A thick pall denying life, it struck at violent sleep, and in some houses the emptiness bruised the backs of small children.

Was it the men's fault that women shrieked blue murder and broke down?

When telephones expanded their world and linked the valleys whose rainforest the women had helped silence, the women sipped tea and ate cakes and talked and talked and talked into a black knob to an answering world. But cars changed the quality of their talking. From the 1960s on, cars ordered a new rhythm. Cars carried the women out of the hills and down through the valleys to the towns where they walked up and down footpaths. They stood in front of butchers' shops and green grocery stores and the haberdashers and department stores and they talked and talked and talked. And they talked into the 70s when the supermarkets began to flourish, and they talked in the aisles with their hands firmly holding their trolleys filled with the food their mothers baked at home. They rejected the companionable sound of wood crackling in fuel stoves. They loved electricity, and talked with relish about a new phenomenon they had read about in the women's magazines, the microwave. When would they be able to get hold of that kind of stove that got cooking over and done with fast? And they talked their way into the carparks and out of the shopping centres of the 80s, sighing Aah! Wheels were good to spin over sealed roads, the rock and dirt tracks, their predecessors remembered with a shudder. And when they had drained themselves of talk, when all the words they knew had flooded from their bodies, they listened to the talk-back radio programs and they watched tee vee sit-coms, learning, studying, investigating how to keep on talking, talking, talking least they should hear the silence moan again.

Words travelled up into the stratosphere and met with the moon. A newer nature grew where the ancient rainforest had been ripped out. The women's noisy talk took on, the emptiness closed over, but scars do not always disappear.

At the university, Jacq wandered down corridors of closed doors and she listened for words being spoken. She sat in tutorial classes and waited to hear a sinewy language. She watched the way words ran in neat lines across pages of the sacred texts of English Literature, ant trails honouring a former vivacity. In silence, she heard only silences.

When Jacq sat in lectures about John Donne's *Valediction*, when she tried to imagine the black sootiness of the brick walls Charles Dickens described, to picture Jon Swift frothing at the mouth as he wrote his tubbed tale, Jacq sailed back to a red roofed house perched above a wide grassy green, drought yellow, watery brown, stinky grey flat where madness whipped and bit and snarled and barked and swung out eventually to whimper. Madness, linked with the elements, may have shrieked at the moon and belied the old poetry. It may, too, have become a new kind of utterance.

Her memory filled with her mother's screechings, Jacq sailed out and round and up and down a picture-book atlas of the world. Whinnied fear lifted her up. On a bubbling cloud, she drifted above the hills where the women twisted whinges and grumbles and complaints in search of words bereft of play, devoid of vigour. Jacq heard them grunting, seeking out the verbal energy to invent a way of saying things, to score their language onto the denuded flats as if the land was green parchment waiting to be smudged.

A speechless contempt gnarled the beauty of the valley she came from. So what? Jacq, writing a valediction in her diary before her father authorised the subdivision of his farm, was well schooled in the belief that humanity is a cause for celebration. As long as the drama's not too discomforting.

Travelling became a way of life. Dawdling round the face of the world, Jacq travelled over the pages of her atlas and back again.

Firstly, she came into the place she travelled to, organised accommodation, found the bank and the information centre, asked questions about the tourist spots, oohed at temples and ahhed down long aisles of things one must shop for. Over the years, she found that roughing it — sleeping in bumpy beds, sharing toilets and showers with other travellers who suffered bouts of dysentery, and having to do her laundry in basins beside decapitated chickens and greasy cooking utensils — lost its glamour. She became more discriminating generally, discovering her fascination with the unfamiliar changed.

No longer did she hover for hours staring at those things that made the place she lived in different from the place she called home. She bought less and less paraphernalia for her boring little flat in Sydney and fewer and fewer clothes and bracelets and rings. But whatever preoccupied her, she discovered herself travelling out of her present place, out of her mind, back into the valley she came from. Wherever she was, high on a parapet at Varberg overlooking a flat sea the Danes fought the Swedes for, picking through a plate of chilli crab at a harbourside restaurant in Penang or Singapore or Macau, or standing half-way down a deep gorge in upstate New York where macho braves historically speared fish, Jacq astro-travelled back to the valley.

She needed no atlas for these journeys. They were mapped, as it were, on her soul. Thus mapped, she remained a valley girl as surely as if she travelled nowhere.

Jacq was not overwhelmed by the detail of incidents. She was not repressed like Kel who daily relived small moments of his childhood. Persistent was the big blue sky and the house nestled behind fruit trees on the hillside above a swampy flat. She remembered the light, a pink gauziness and something finer like spun gold, washing over the land after the thunderstorms of a summer's afternoon. In her head she saw the fast tangling of shadows around colours before the sky and the earth tumbled into each other at nightfall. She smelt a dankness, too, and there was the pressured silence of dew wetting earth, of rain weighing down the foliage of trees and bushes, beading in the cupped petals of flowers and pearling between the spores of coloured mosses and elaborate fungi. Too much rain, too much sun, too much fecundity. From Penang, she wrote in a letter to Kel, *A lot of things here rot from too much of everything*, knowing he would then understand the kind of place she was walking through.

Maps.
Atlases.

Spinning round the equator drawn around the globe. You need only look at the quasi-adventurous spots on a tourists' map of the world to find the hypersensitive traveller. Sometimes they plunge forwards into Romanticism, all part of the pleasure of leaving routine business for somnolent leisure, parodying the movies and the ads beamed into the world's living rooms, sloughing a skin for a more admirable one.

There she is, Jacq, pronged by Poseidon in 1982. Although his hard eye fixed on Madagascar, his trident prodded Penang. A fish flew a perfect round leap from the Indian Ocean side of the island towards Nias, an island off the west coast of Sumatra. She had been given the Penang address of an accommodating Australian, Patrick Dreher, in Bangkok, and there she is, walking away from the punishing trident and the leaping fish down Jalan Dunn to his house.

She had walked all day. She walked down Aceh Street, Armenia Street and Wharf Road where men leered at the lone white woman. She wandered through their curiosity to the Khoo Kongsi and the Indian mosque. She stopped at a stall for a sugarcane juice and a moment to mop at the perspiration trickling between her breasts and wetting her dress under her arms and at the centre of her back. She lifted her hat to wipe at the band of wet hair gluing her forehead. Her head absorbed the heat, the light, and reminded itself to compare this light with another light. Her body travelled as if it was independent and on the ground.

The world pictured as segmented light troubled her far less than comprehending it analytically. That way, she could look at how much the Snake Temple had changed since 1970. Back then, it was a garish building surrounded by an overgrowth of jungle. Snakes slithered round all the fixtures and dangled precariously above her when she hoisted her skirt in the toilet block. In 1982, she looked at a naked thing abandoned on a dust plain and unadorned by snakes. When she stood in the changed Snake Temple, she absorbed into herself a new, and strange, patterning of light.

A lot of Penang had changed in twelve years.

From the bus window she watched Tamil boys walk under trees at the edge of a *kampong* set a short distance from the highway bulleting to the airport. A cow walked with the boys, a goat bleated at them, and a few turkeys gobbled at the boys' knees. One boy walked across a grassless stretch buckling under the midday heat. Twirling a stick, the boy pushed at a cow's rump, coaxing the lumbering beast up and onto the road in front of the bus. He pushed the cow into the flow of traffic that widened each day, drawing the *kampong* closer to another way of doing things.

Jacq wandered, her mind absent, perhaps lying with the Buddha reclining on one side of the island, perhaps high in the hills where mistresses waited for their wealthy playboy lovers, perhaps low along the tidal flats where *kampong* houses slid into the muddy waters that used to be filled with spawning fish, perhaps, perhaps, perhaps …

She listened to the world as if its sounds were strange. The morning's rain, a heavy long pouring, gave way to a rustling, a humming. If she stopped her breathing, she heard a rush of water falling, a restless stillness cascading somewhere in the jungle up a hill.

At mid-afternoon, after the muezzin's call to prayer, she lent over a plate of curry and *pan* near the university, and she listened to an eerie quiet. The eeriness, fractured above the sound of cars speeding to and from the anxieties of humanity, floated through the heat and the humidity. And the eeriness lifted her up. She kind of floated, bewitched. Her body moved into the pearliness of the late afternoon where she was swallowed under a blanketing soundlessness.

Jacq looks down the long drive at a yellow stucco house sliding off stumps ridden with wood louse into a time-lapsing garden. The flowering trees and bold crotons and green vines twist to snare a pale almond light falling over the front porch and the leadlight windows. The walls shudder. The doors, dropping off their hinges, and the curtains, pleating over window spaces, collapse. As if gripped by a sickening dream, the whole house curves round itself to muzzle an agony in its wavering walls.

When she becomes aware her body is motionless half-way down Patrick's drive, Jacq touches her mouth to know with her fingertips that the lineaments are in place. She spreads her hands over her face, and she peers through the bars her stretched fingers make at changes another part of herself can see are too rapid to believe.

A shiver spins up a massive ansenna tree. Its branches

quiver. The dappled shade on the ground shies and shrinks. Long blades of yellowed grass ripple towards the house. In a strange bending of rays, its walls straighten up, its paint brightens. The brightness stuns an incandescence. Red roof tiles slap down, the windows snap to, and the curtains, gathering a breeze, balloon, then slowly fall in soft pleats. Humming cicadas underscore the silence, and a feeble music, perhaps a dance band wobbling under a heavy gramophone needle, underlaps the stillness.

A curtain sweeps sideways, the music stops and a young woman's face thrusts beside the bunched up lace. She stares down the drive. The curtain falls over the window, a hand pushes it aside, and again the young woman thrusts her face beside the bunched up lace.

Anxiety makes the young woman look fragile. Tragically drawn, her eyes distend as if they themselves are large tears dropping on her cheeks. She stares. At Jacq. Through Jacq.

All of a sudden her lips slide back to reveal her gums. Her lipless mouth opens, and a ghastly sighing hisses and whinnies and striates the yellowishness. Thin white arms stream through the window down the drive.

A death's head travelling behind ribboning arms swirls around and under and through the shade, its doleful moaning and frenzied screeching swinging round Jacq's head like a creature flying from hell. The old tree shudders terror into its roots.

Cowardice hobbles Jacq's legs. Alone, she hears herself listening to leaves rustling and teeth chattering, but several minutes pass before she knows the teeth are hers. Painfully, her body stirs.

Her ears hurt. A shrill woman's voice orders tea.

The shape of a man blacks out the light.

The woman, the one whose voice is high, its timbre loose, wraps a length of cloth around Jacq's shoulders and she presses something to Jacq's lips, something smooth and thin and suddenly hot. It's Meena, Patrick's housekeeper, pressing hot sweet tea to Jacq's lips. Jacq feels the liquid trickling down her gullet. She senses nerve endings, from her lips to the pit of her stomach, leap, shocked back to life by the liquid heat.

"Shocked back to life," Jacq says. She's surprised by the gravelly depth of her voice .

The man says, "What?"

He fills the doorway of an oblong room. The light behind his head casts shadows over his features, but she remembers, groping with difficulty back into a time-frame dominated by the continuous present, she was visiting Patrick Dreher's house before everything bent sideways and she lost her way.

Patrick half expects to be dismissed by Meena for interfering with women's business. He knows she considers her gender is distinguished and made more mysterious from the brute habits of men by sensitivities that may be advantages or obstacles, depending on contextual interpretation. That he found Jacq standing on his doorstep, a white gibbering lunatic, and that he sought her advice, did not alter Meena's disdain of his ability to understand what caused Jacq's distress. Meena's babbling "You've had a shock, quite nasty really. It's the time, the time. Tuan Patrick cannot you see? She saw. You saw. A lady? A young lady? At the window? A ghost lady every Dissember like I said, Tuan Patrick, a ghost lady lives every Dissember," did not persuade him to take her reasoning seriously.

Over Meena's brown eyes a yellow flecked membrane stretches to a pale yellow rim, dimming their lustre but not decreasing their size. The pupils at their centre skid crazily into the pale face of Patrick's visitor. Meena's small strong hands brush hair off the woman's forehead. The clammy pink skin alarms her fingers. She understands Jacq lacks earth, lacks the will to withstand fear.

Holding a teacup between two warming hands, Jacq's tears press her eyelids. Shame, that she should cry, appals her body. She hands the cup to the space in front of her.

Someone grasps it before it falls to the floor. In the same moment Jacq buries her head in the folds of the sari tossed over Meena's shoulder. She sobs convulsively.

Meena rocks her like a baby.

When night falls, and from her vantage point beneath the giant rainforest tree blackening Patrick's driveway, Gillian winces with irritation at a placid face gazing as if entranced by Patrick's fastidious attentions. She judges the compliance of the face's owner is assured.

Gillian's bottom lip buttons under her puckering top one. With circumspect calm, she walks briskly up the front steps to the porch. When she knocks and then opens the front door and walks into the room, her ironic eye catches Jacq's wretched fear. A graceful rhythm takes hold of Gillian's limbs, and she moves as if her body rids itself of a cautionary foreboding. Inclining her head over Jacq, offering her solicitations, Gillian Hindmarsh would charm.

Jacq, eyes glassy from fear and with embarrassment, moves to grasp Gillian's offered hand. But, discouragingly, Gillian's face suddenly distorts and looms over her. Gillian's hand slowly extends, the fingers weirdly lengthening as her face weirdly smiles and her eyes weirdly tip down the sides of her face. The ghostly woman rushes behind Gillian's forever bending body. The creature pushes back the sash at the window, pushes back the sash of yesteryear, pushes back the sash that's no longer there. Jacq shivers. She begins to stammer that there's a ghost in the room when the woman at the window swims into the night, uttering a diabolic cry that bites deep into Jacq's terrified sub-consciousness.

Abandoning the idiot Jacq, Gillian walks to the window to look down the long drive to the roadway. She peers at the blackness under the large ansenna tree. She examines the way the light from the house fades and loses its effectiveness up the drive to the street.

Patrick rushes about with hot drinks and face cloths

soaked in lily-of-the-valley toilet water. Gillian, after what seems to be a long time, leans against the windowsill and watches Patrick placing and replacing the damp scented cloths on Jacq's head. She watches them both without really seeing them. She says as if to herself, although she is hopeful they will hear her, "I thought I saw a ghost." But Patrick is distracted. He is not listening to her. Rather he is hoping to hear Meena begin her chanting in the pavilion behind the big house. He has come to know her evening prayer, accompanied by tropical balminess, imposed a certain peace.

Tiredly swatting a lone mosquito with the free end of her sari, Meena prepares to pray to Sri Ganes for a quick end to this December. Tuan Patrick's guest whipped up quite a charm bedevilling the poor Missee, the house ghost. Meena's mother told her Missee's aunt and uncle left her to fend for herself against the Japanese, bad Missee, running off to be with her young man and missing the boat when the English saved themselves, leaving behind all the people they lived and worked with for many years, circumstance overriding the goodness at the bottom of their hearts, bad circumstance making wrong things happen, bad karma spinning around eventually to tip right, to balance, to bring harmony to all, including Patrick's woman, Gillian, and the pale eyed Jacq Dark who Meena noticed were as similar as they were dissimilar the way cousins can be, and she saw they were awkward with each other as if a family feud had kept them apart and that they did not really know each other or like each other, but the poor Missee had shown herself to both of them, and Meena touches her heart and her forehead as the prayerful do in bewildering moments like these, for she believes Gillian is not properly a woman and she knows Jacq's mind to be quite unsound.

Sky, a vacancy above, yawns.
A vacancy within widens.
The immensity buckles. Slightly.

Meena, so passive to her karma, keels into a dreamless sleeping.

♓

4.   *and how to see sunshine*

At a breakfast stall on Lorong Chulia with the municipal and bank clerks of Penang, Gillian Hindmarsh indulges a passion for *roti çanai*, curry sauce and sweet milky tea. Patrick Dreher, her lover, watches her tear the roti and dab it in the sauce. Disdainful of this spiced breakfast, he leans back on his stool and plays his fingers on his belt buckle, and he rocks forwards with questions about Gillian's cousin, Jacq Dark.

"Yes! We're cousins! Her father was my mother's brother."

"I went to school with her. Same year. Same class for some subjects, BUT! We had very little to do with each other. Mother's orders!"

"Yes! Mother's orders!" Fumbling with the rolled roti, she flicks up the words, "Something to do with a cake recipe."

From the beginning, Gillian remembered Jacq was the target of the boys' bad jokes on the old school bus.

Her long boney wrists stalk the air like the knees of a tall water bird. When they fall across the table, Gillian's earrings swing and jangle. Watching her quickly wet another strip of roti with curry sauce, Patrick asks as if repeating, "*Cake* recipe? What's this about a *cake* recipe?" Her lips hesitate before she allows, "Jacq was weird. *Painfully* thin, she was. Painfully thin! And ... WEIRD!"

Patrick's occasional irritation with Gillian's emphatic turn-of-phrase resurfaces to level with a memory of her mouth tantalising his cock. He flinches slightly and shifts his legs, directing his gaze across the black heads of the clerks bobbing up and down over their roti çanai and sweet milky tea breakfasts where flits a shadow of last night's encounter with Jacq's shy eyes. Rather like those of a trusting yet frightened puppy, they arrested his for a bare moment.

Affecting detachment, he talks on about Jacq. "Once lived here. For about four years. Several years ago."

Gillian, tearing another piece of roti, hears Patrick's story about her cousin teaching English and having an affair with a Malay student she planned to marry. First dunking the torn wedge in curry sauce, dabbing, twisting, mopping, she then carries it with gusto to her hungering mouth. Back on the school bus, back then, opinion denounced Jacq's thinness. Girls were supposed to wrench their belts in like grocers' string round their school tunics. Skinny girls like Jacq who did not have to do that had lessons in humility and 'knowin' what's good for'em' to learn. And her eyebrows were real and not pencilled in the way normal girls drew in theirs.

Teachers, too, were dismissive. They tired of Jacq's striving to do well and better than well, and they took sadistic delight in admonishing her for any failed attempts, her awkwardness excusing their lack of sympathy. They forgot the girl whose pale eyes shone with an intensity that split her face in two. Perhaps it was that bisected look that fuelled their contempt.

When Patrick confides "She called it off. The marriage. Family pressure. His family. The aunts, I gather, and the grandmother ... They wanted her to have a clitoridectomy," information that is for him scandalous, Gillian snorts "Well! One way to get rid of her!"

Startled, Patrick stares at Gillian's face, a devilish mask angled to the sun, greased and yellowed lips lopsided and actively chewing. Horrified, he flings his chair back and strides to the lane's corner and turns down Lorong Pasar.

In front of a favourite *nyonya* restaurant, he reacts to Gillian's affection for him by kicking the footpath and cursing her name. Then he plunges one fist into his other. Reality, shining with the sunshine, dries up whatever garbage the crows may have left spilling from the kitchen refuse dumped underneath a dragon's wing.

Pausing at a hawker's stall for a lime juice, Patrick considers, with a touch of chagrin, Gillian, calm in the night until her dreams woke her, abjured mystery. She said she never wanted to lose her sanity to the neuroses of an indulgent love affair.

And yet!

Rapidly draining his glass, Patrick recalls the sepia photograph of a woman in a slipper satin gown, the charm of nostalgia framed for Gillian's bedside table. Rather like a publicity shot of Greta Scaachi advertising *Heat and Dust*, a movie set in the 30s. Or was it the 20s when too much girlishness lost a young woman her Empire? Patrick knew the film to be a voluptuous woman's love story, and he believes Gillian keeps the photograph by her bed to remind herself that this was what she wanted and that this was what she must avoid.

Jacq, well, yes, she was intriguing but the Jacq he remembers, is the one with the fingers fluttering and landing with the lightness of a moth on his arm accompanied by a breathy "Aaah! Patrick!" Jacq. Her shoulders hunched around a defeated admission that she was "On my way home. From a failed love affair!" That Jacq exuded desire. Both the glass in her hand and her skirt twirled. She swallowed a girlish laugh. "In my case, love's an allergy." Before he could blink, she drew in a sob, and she whispered, seemingly not for hearing, "Thinning already thin skin."

What did she mean? Was she afflicted by an uncommon ailment? Or was she one of those perpetual tragic heroines?

Thumping the empty glass on the stall counter with a nod and a half-smile ending in a near wink, he moves to step forward. Thrown off his balance by the memory of those fluttering fingers and her sighing advice that "Aaah! Patrick! There's a ghost in your house," he almost looses his footing, almost stumbles into a deep drain running between the footpath and the road. She was, she attested, a medium sensitive to the spirit world.

More than melodramatic, he concedes. A bit frightening. However, Patrick will pander his curiosity. He is inclined to take life with two hands. By the hard sun of a new day, Patrick may be seen to be a young man more afraid of living uneventfully than one who retreats behind cushioned domesticities. If last night's memories of the woman, Jacq, excite him, it's because, unlike Gillian, she will, he knows, be ardently responsive. When he carefully peers into the deep drain he almost fell into, he recognises his excitement is accompanied by a lot of gut warnings about clinging neurotic women. Patrick is too polite, too well brought up, to agree frankly with his sub-conscious understanding that Jacq looked like she would be a more gymnastic fuck than Gillian.

He decides to ask her over. And immediately Patrick spies his car. Sun, expanding the tropically yellow sky, emblazons heat waves shimmering around the old cream Peugeot. It looked stupidly abandoned, not simply stationary.

Sitting on a disenfranchised school teachers' chair, tucking into her roti çanai breakfast, Gillian feigns nonchalance. For the very instant Patrick abruptly walked off, several municipal and bank clerks, without pausing in their conversations or their breakfasting, directed solemn and lewd stares at that creature of the sex they defined as White Western Woman, therefore not really a woman at all, nevertheless a lone person of womanly shape and possibilities, a woman thing bereft of male company, therefore stripped of her identity, therefore without any status, an object, a thingummy, an aberration — an amputated limb in need of its host (male) body — therefore available and thus and therefore a corruptibly corrupt corrupted bit of flesh.

A jangling of keys burst through the quick mounting pall. The violent clang of metal doors twists heads.

Two Chinese youths back their Honda motor scooters out of a narrow doorway. They straddle the saddles and, behind a fart of blue smoke, they glide to the street corner.

Gillian stares after their easy disappearance.

Being the object of rude curiosity is not her idea of a good way to start the day. With a pout, she prepares to stride with confidence after the motor scooters. Then a greeting bowls across the humming voices and the leery eyes. "Miss Hindmarsh! Good morning! Miss Hindmarsh! How are you today?" From a rickety chair, his breakfast plate slicked clean of curry sauce, a young man smiles with slight insolence. "Will you be working in the Library again, Miss Hindmarsh?"

Her identity made known, the other men lose interest. They continue to discuss the exchange rate, what the devil that Mr Big-time Wang Shi-zheng thinks he's doing, the influx of Korean labour for road-building and channel dredging which in 1982 was displacing the local Malays, and whose family funeral, wedding, birthing, naming they attended a day or two ago. The young man, cognisant of this, beams with cheerful if overt cynicism.

Gillian answers his greeting with more suspicion than decorum. She has no desire to display too much familiarity. She resists her country girl's big smile. She arches her eyebrow and nods at the library assistant. "Shall see you there, Mr Mukhapadai. After nine." She hears her voice. It rings, too shrill at the edges.

The library assistant, no longer enjoying rescuing this woman who was never very friendly to him, responds with a grave if sly nod of his own. She may be a scholar, an historian, white and not bad to look at, but after all is said done, she is merely a woman.

Relationships between library staff and scholars may be complementary if not spoiled by social convention. After all, many academics spend their lives loving librarians. It is a relationship founded on the principle that to search every known avenue for knowledge — the way different writers recorded the date of a well-known event for example, the naming of a river by an invading force who could not understand nor were interested in learning the indigenous people's language, or perhaps the construction of sentences written by a famous novelist during her climacteric — is both a fundamental joy and an important reminder of humanity.

Librarians classify knowledge for improved accessibility. With a glance at the cover page, at the table of contents and the index if there is one, and at the blurb, rules about subject headings, keywords and descriptors are applied to the book in hand. The world, according to its classifiers, is segmented, and the greater part of its knowledge agglomerated in North America and Europe, including England. The florid complexities of Asia and Africa made classification unworkable, best ignored as the refined do any potential riot.

And escaping the classification system altogether are the twists and the inter-connectedness of multi-cultural thought, that twentieth century mongrelisation graduates from Schools of Information Science may not easily encode.

Keywords prescribed in 1982 will be inadequate for future comprehension when searches down tubes and beamed from satellite to personal computer to laptop along conduits of microchips to microdots will require a singular passion. Hidden behind alpha- and numeric-codes, information will be buried, waiting for someone with the flexibility of mind to link thought with thought, word to word, thoughts into words and back again, serendipitously finding a gem, a chance surprise, a depository of forgotten knowledge. We do circle around ourselves, we humans.

Floundering through an unwieldy and idiosyncratic card file system at the Dewan Sri Penang, Gillian yearned for automation. To compensate for the municipal library's inadequacy, she developed an old-fashioned dependence on Oh!, a trial and a blessing!, an asset and a liability! — Mr Mukhapadai, the library assistant. He was good at keeping an eye out for the miscatalogued and the incompletely accessioned, true, true, because he wanted to share small wonders and learned observations. Mr Mukhapadai yearned, not for automation, but for a slower pace when time was consumed pleasantly in conversation.

His diligence served her well. He gave her bundles of leaflets from the Chinese associations, but their statements mixed with inference imposed inexact silences. He found, lodged between two fat volumes, a pamphlet containing a description of a bombed mansion written in the late 40s by a doughty member of the Ladies' Auxiliary Guild of St George's Church of England. It literally fell into his hands, and he passed it on to her with reserved pleasure.

A local history he knew, tucked at the back of a tennis club bulletin, may have been brief, but it threw an interesting light in a parenthetic paragraph on the origin of a certain architect who had worked in India before residing in Georgetown just before the War. 'The War' was always the Second World War, a time of great privation and suffering for the sleepy island town, a time of destroying, not of building. As such, some may regard that period in human history described as the Second World War as not directly relevant to Gillian's history.

If she were in possession of more imagination, would Gillian have known to search for a depository at the back of the shop on Lorong Chulia the two Chinese boys burst from? Nothing existed on microfiche or in a data base to suggest she should look there. Is the better historiographical tool, access to technical resources, losing its potency to pure chance? Without doubt, Gillian could never have guessed those boys' uncle and father pilfered the vacated British residences after the Europeans evacuated under cover of darkness before the dawn of December 14, 1941.

Predicting there would be shortages of paper and other mundane items, the brothers planned to sell their loot later for a good price. Under a broken planter's chair, they stored boxes stuffed full of papers, newspapers, women's magazines, sheet music, radio sets, cameras, film canisters, photograph albums and framed portraits. And sewing machines.

At the sound of the occupiers' bark, the unfortunate uncle attracted undue attention. Although no one could explain how repairing bicycles was a subversive activity, the boys' father understood his brother was tortured and executed for this crime. Taking this example as fair warning, he slipped away to the mainland, hiding in the jungle for the years of the occupation.

From his vantage point high in a large tree strangled by vines, he observed demons whose appetite for atrocities he knew to be insatiable. Storms brewed, ravishing hope with violence and terror, but sun, and the bitter brilliance of sky, refreshed the earth, and it smelt wet.

After the War was over and he made his way back to the place he liked to call home, his brother's voice, reverberating inside his head, directed him to keep away from the pilfered goods at the back of the shop on Lorong Chulia. Working as if his brother's body continued to warm the space beside his, he left the stuff to rot under the broken planter's chair. He added to it, a crazy mound of tins, bolts, screws and nails, broken bicycles, bits of wire twisted with electrical flex and telegraphic equipment growing more ungainly. Every conceivable species of circumtropical muncher feasted underneath the mound on the damp and mouldy remains of an era brutally ended, not to be revisited.

The boys' father looked to the future. Borrowing recklessly from the Wang bank, he shared with his spectral brother a new enthusiasm for a technology that would reduce the world to a microdot.

Under the shop's roof, paper, ingested, dropped as another substance. Lives, fragmented on celluloid, corroded in canisters and crumbled under cockroach shit. History, for that's the story, missed a clue.

Time tick-tocked. Echoed, and clattered under a banner billowing over nothing but empty space. A screen may have draped across a naked wall, an after-dinner audience surely watched home-movies.

No one but an unsuspecting wayfarer or burglar or perhaps a cleaner would ever have reason to investigate the garbage under the planter's chair. The old movies will remain unclassified, uncatalogued, nor will they ever be processed for storage on an optical disc.

One canister may have impressed Gillian if she had been able to see it. It contained a flickering home-movie of two women. One grey afternoon, they bent over a low runnel. Crouched. And from their squat position, they turned in unison to face a recording eye with something held high between fingers. The outline of flowers may have been discerned, but the light behind the objects was too bright, smudging their shape.

The action was repeated several times. Then the women stood abruptly and faced the camera like girls queuing before classes at school. The younger one clasped her hands behind her back, quickly releasing them to cover her laughing mouth. She seemed to quiver and rock about as if she was silly.

The older woman cocked her head askance and hunched her shoulders, drawing a giggle into herself.

The camera lingered on the women. They stopped giggling, their self-consciousness giving way to submission. The older one composed herself by standing to attention and brushing down her skirt, the loose cloth folding and pleating around her. Her hair, sitting like a cap on her head, gleamed.

The younger one looked away as if she was bored with standing still before the camera. Then there was an abrupt break. The relentless eye suddenly swerved after the direction of her gaze, hopping round the garden beds which were filled with hibiscus and poinsettia and orchids and allemande and caladium and large elk horns. It flashed past a porch and a garage. A leadlight window glittered, the focus lost to a sudden loss of interest or anger.

Gillian may have identified in the younger woman the subject of the sepia photograph she had framed for her bedside table. She may also have recognised the house from its parts. It looked very like the one Patrick lived in on Jalan Dunn.

In the library, Gillian settles down for yet another day among the trackings of thysanuran insects scored through newspaper clippings, building and development applications, minutes of meetings and bureaucratic memoranda. She enters a globe, her concentration on the documents in hand commendable. She had neatly resolved and managed to by-pass Patrick's disruption of her breakfasting habits with his curiosity about her cousin, Jacq.

But she was troubled by night dreams. In them, a terrible face spun under spidery whorls. From its lipless mouth, a singing, a sighing, exhaled. She thought it was the woman whose photograph she found in the library, the one she framed and put beside her bed.

Gillian straightens, and rotates her arm to release a knotted pain under her shoulder blade. She throws her head back, throws off the thrall of the ghostly woman.

Holding a book between his two hands, Mr Mukhapadai walks into her bunker to ask her if she would like iced tea at the mid-morning break. She is annoyed by his intrusion, less by the interruption than by his manner, which she deems is patronising. She hopes her face does not redden. With anger. At him. And at herself for responding at all to the way he glides and enlargens in the space he takes for himself. A fear of her inextinguishable desire for an obsessive love affair, for Romance, that high plane of Western extravagance opposing apathy, grips her. She cannot get away from the fact that Mr Mukhapadai attracts her. With pitiless rapidity, her body zings as if it wants to offer itself mindlessly, herself somehow absent.

She sees her reflection spinning through her head, demanding less reason, less rational belief, and a weariness wells from the dusty floor. Not looking at him directly, she addresses the room. Gillian evinces her desire is to experiment with form. She states her ambition is to escape the perimeters of the conventional historical narrative.

Her voice alterior, she hears herself say, "I may write an adequate thesis from these researches. But I wish I could face myths and give them flesh."

Light pours through a window high above the book stacks, blurring the figure of Mr Mukhapadai but not his dazzling smile. She does not respond. Adamant that she should maintain her scholarly appearance, Gillian gives him a sidelong look she hopes will put an end to the possibility of any blandishments. She affects a knowing and discouraging smirk when she says, "Well, Mr Mukhapadai! What have we here!?"

His smile widens. And the sun, ascendant in his horoscope, irradiates all around him.

♓

5. *passions*

Mukhapadai.

A good name for a librarian, suggesting a respect for learning, therefore a spiritualism making his a better kind of life. Badul, sighing in his newly wed's surprised sleep, wears it well.

Mei-mei is very fair. Even so, when he announced his intention to marry her, his mother screamed abuse at him for punishing her with a future of mixed race grandchildren. She demanded a suitable monetary compensation in the form of a dowry. When the chips were down, his mother was exactingly traditional.

Badul fumbles love for adoration, confusing pedantry with attentiveness. Habitually, he rests his cheek on Mei-mei's thin shoulder, drifts into a landscape high above a glittering sea, and wakes violently, wishing Gillian Hindmarsh would leave his sleep sacred.

Badul Mukhapadai draws his young wife into the spoon his body makes.

Gillian is sitting with Patrick on the five footway outside a shophouse just round the corner from Penang Road. Patrick is sipping tea and eating a bun with red pork filling. Shi-zheng, a glass of beer at his elbow, looks over the top of the newspaper he is reading to watch the thin legs of the black lacquered chair wobble when Patrick tilts back. He has seen this pair. He knows the woman studies history, and he remembers Patrick is renting an old house from him, an investment he plans to demolish.

Flipping back her hand, Gillian is enumerating the stylistic origins of the tiles decorating this shophouse, from the multi-coloured floor patterns to the floral ebullience under the windows beside an elaborately painted doorway. Shi-zheng is surprised by the energy of her speech. He would not be astonished if Patrick suddenly tipped forward to stop her energetic mouth with a kiss. In the USA, at university, a young man did that to his garrulous girlfriend right in front of Shi-zheng, and he wished he could do it. But to do that, to stop a flow of words with a firm and passionate kiss, he would have to believe he was acting in the movies. He would have to know that a camera was about to zoom in on him from somewhere. That he was a heartthrob. Like Warren Beatty.

The newspaper in his hand bends. With a slight tremor of unease about his prowess or the lack of it, he is aware Patrick stops chewing. Shi-zheng, knowing he must not stare, likes to see the way Patrick's eyes crinkle with a thought circling a thousand miles away from Gillian's informed chat. Her lecture! About these five footways, footpaths with arched ceilings, blendings of the Chinese with adaptations from British India. "But I don't have the languages", she is saying, her earrings swinging and her bracelets jangling, "to access the building plans that may be in Arabic, Tamil, Jawi ... Which I am sure are buried in the Archives. Somewhere."

And then, she says, one hand swiftly gesturing towards heaven, "There's all the stuff about GARdens!" Sinking her teeth into a red bean paste bun, Gillian mumbles, "There were movements of plants, migrations of plants, going with and following the people migrating from one place to another." Swallowing a lump of white dough, her hand waves in the observation Patrick has heard her repeat often, "Extending memory. Adding to ... Connecting memories." Then, through a full mouth, she says, "Of one place to another place. In big loops. Like wheels." Her head jerks as she gulps down mouthfuls of bean paste bun.

Shi-zheng folds his paper shut. He stands up quietly and he walks round the tables to Patrick. Greeting him, he offers his hand. Patrick falls forward from his precarious tilt. He catches Shi-zheng's hand. As he stands, shaking hands and blushing, he manages to say, "G'day!"

Shi-zheng, inclining his head and taking a departing backwards step, nods at Gillian. Unsmiling, she looks straight through him.

Gillian is obsessed.

Detail, the emblems pictured on a tile, the different patterns of rattan plaiting the seat of a chair, the shape and colour of a bottle, or the line of stitches quilting rich silk, sends her into raptures.

Patrick ignores it. Badul wants more of it.

And Shi-zheng?

The past slithers into Gillian's everyday. She may be studying buildings to avoid confronting herself, and she would have to do that if she studied the history of the people working in the buildings.

Badul Mukhapadai guesses this. He has a shrewd idea what she might have been if she had not been to university. He senses a woman carrying a bucket and a small gardening fork in one gloved hand, in the palm of her other a seedling. She bore a resemblance to an Englishwoman from a book he studied for an examination. He may have seen her likeness in Wales where he was sent to study librarianship. Or did she resemble a calendar painting of a real woman tending camellias? But when she stood still to run her eye out to the sky's meeting with earth or water, Badul recognises the Australian, that sun centred mind and body searching for another sort of spiritualism found under roots, rustling and murmuring down creek banks.

Gillian instructs herself not to indulge impediments like fleeting liaisons with the Mr Mukhapadais of the world. Badul is left with no doubt about this. Her obsessions run across the bungalow, the British Indian adaptation of the *bangaloo* of Bengal, and how representatives of other colonial styles found their way into Penang. She educates Patrick to see how the depth of the verandahs and the wooden decorative features of some of Penang's houses were developments on the original. She explained how the *balik kampung* of Malaya began to make good its influence in parts of Australia in that deep space under the ground floor some people used as a kind of fern house or a storage dump. Others walled it up, and put in a shower and a toilet and rooms for gardening tools and fertilisers. Or, behind lattice, hammocks and shelves where books and magazines mouldered.

There was a memory, she theorises, in the form of architecture, and it sometimes crossed the seas.

Believing more in the amorous fictions of the cinema than Gillian's investigations into the origins of stylistic detail, Patrick, poorly acting patience, camouflages his boredom.

Whereupon Gillian paints a utopian picture of a house somehow mixed up with her family, a tall house in Ballina, an east coast beach town in Australia. Standing on a hilly corner, the house looked nothing like the others in the street. They were eaveless, red brick monstrosities with aluminium framed windows sparkling in a sun that fired the interiors. The old house was walled in and there were windows and doors. "In there," she is saying to Patrick. "Under its high exterior staircase, under there, there was a shower and a hammock." She did not mention the peep-hole in the wall of the shower room where she found one of her mother's cousins, an older man with boiled eyes, buttoning up his fly one day. At that time, when her prepubescent body pouted all over, her skin went clammy, shocked that he might have watched her shower after a swim. But Gillian rids memory of the fumbling cousin. She kills his shadow in her head, and she fills the blank spot his annihilation opens up by pointing out how the ground floor disappeared under a verandah jutting "… like an apron across the front of a house. Like Sarawak houses." And the supporting timber posts and wooden pillars decorating the verandah of the older bungalows built down on Ballina's river plain were like those on the Selangor style houses.

"Gardens," she says, chin high, "make the difference."

(She does get carried away.)

Gillian grew up with her sister, Fi, in the Hindmarsh farmhouse at Newrybar, a nothing of a place high above the Pacific Ocean — above Ballina and Byron Bay. Its excessive beauty dared Gillian's mother, Muriel Hindmarsh, to choke on days of dreaming nothing. Driven by a fervour, singular enough to be religious, and like many others in those hilly farms, Muriel circumcised her life with secateurs and pruning saws.

Muriel attempted a cool elegance drawn from the pages of the women's magazines and the soapies screened on television, of lawns and hybrid natives surrounded at their feet by neat clusters of alyssum and ageratum, white bricks and daisies. She let Grandma Hindmarsh's prize rose garden of old perfumed varieties grow rank. Before she will die, Muriel will completely raze the wisteria with the plaited trunks arching over the gate opening into the chookpen, and she will chop out the date palm with its lower trunk entirely covered by pink waxies. But she will not quite get round to pulling out the blue hydrangeas growing under the big kitchen window. Or the crazy path leading to the old dunny collapsing under a passion fruit vine.

Muriel, watching Gillian gaze dreamily at nothing, did not see how her daughter was sifting through her brain ideas about how the world on top of the hills at Newrybar seemed to thwart change even though the news broadcast on the radio insisted many things were changing.

Shivering in the early morning, Gillian heard the rooster crow when gold light burst across the sky to fire the tree tops. Her body understood, when it felt the morning's blast, the stillness in the earth. Pressing her hands between her knees, Gillian saw, in the dawn song and in those other more ordinary things she lived with, that history lost a torn out page. Things turned circle when history recorded for posterity the big bangs described on the radio news as 'eventful' and 'advances' and 'progress'.

She grew up with gardens. Formally, she learned gardens have their special history, told by the species of plants selected for decoration or for more functional purposes. Anecdotally, she knew every plant in her mother's garden represented the day when it was given as a cutting, and the person who gave it. All plants, Gillian believed, were stories, some little, some momentous.

She also believed the story of gardens was told by the style of dress chosen for tending both earth and plants.

Muriel wore misshapen straw hats, the likes of which Gillian never saw in shops. She did not know where she got them from. Muriel worked in faded floral shifts, garments worn to church when they were new dresses.

In her walks around Penang, Gillian compared the choices of plants grown in the island's old gardens and the old gardens of the Far North Coast of New South Wales — white lilies, tiger lilies, zinnias, asters, balsams, orchids, sunflowers, marigolds, black-eyed susie, gardenias, roses, African daisies, hollyhocks and bougainvillea.

"History delivered A *House and Garden* influence. Settings, Patrick, for the gestures of the lovers we see on the big screen. Patrick! Remember that funny old film *The Letter?* Bette Davis? The garden, the big leafed plants? And lots of others?" But Patrick's droll smile extinguishes any chance of developing a discussion on the subject. She smiles over the rim of her tea glass — squints into the elbow room Patrick's kind of affection gives her.

Badul, if ever he should have Gillian's horticultural sentiments explained to him, would shake his head. He longed for a long chat with her about the settlement history of Penang, to share his knowledge about people and events. Without hesitation, he would elaborate on the little he knew about gardens merely to entertain her.

Wang Shi-zheng, rubbing his forehead, worries a series of computations through his brain.

Fish under the sea nose stones and trim weeds to create a gardened bower for a fertile mate to swim through.

There was that home movie.

No music played for the new garden on Dunn Street when, billowing steadily, a screen was draped across a wall.

Two women, one grey afternoon, walked between new beds. They crouched and, from their squat position, they faced a camera with something held high between fingers. When the older woman stood abruptly and faced the camera like a girl queuing before classes at school, the younger one imitated her. The two of them repeated the squatting and the standing to attention several times. Then the younger one clasped her hands behind her back. She burst into laughter. She quickly released her hands to cover her laughing mouth. She seemed to rock about as if she was silly.

The older woman cocked her head and hunched her shoulders, drawing a giggle into herself.

There was Rose. And Margaret Willoughby. Cedric, the uncle of one and the husband of the other, crouched behind the camera. He was recording Rose's first day in Penang.

The women giggled self-consciously. Aunt Margaret was the first to compose herself. She stood to attention and she brushed down her skirt, the loose cloth folding and pleating around her.

Rose did not know where to look. She did not want to look bored. She wanted to appear grateful. Then a servant announced afternoon tea. Cedric bounced. His head popped up from under the black cloth and he spied a tray of pastries. He tripped over a leg of the tripod. The camera wobbled and heaved upwards, angling precariously at the porch. A leadlight window glittered.

Cedric Willoughby had an appetite for pastries.

Rose, eating one of these dainty cakes, admired the graceful oval framing the porch. The afternoon light struck a ruby redness in the lead light windows. The garden, newly planted with hibiscus, poinsettia, orchids, allemande, caladium and large elkhorns, promised elegance. Sinking into her surroundings, Rose heard from some streets away the low rumble of a bullock cart, the call of a hawker selling curry puffs, and the roar of a shouting crowd at a sporting event broadcast on a wireless. A car hummed passed the gate.

She lent against a stillness. That's when Rose felt the emptiness in her remind her that, without a mother or a father to share the day, she did not belong anywhere. The sadness rolled sideways. An insight widened, beckoning a quality of calm at once so spiritual and sensual she cried.

Badul Mukhapadai stirs.

Mei-mei's arms circle his neck.

♓

6.   *the house on Jalan Dunn*

In the end, there will be no house. Eventually a condominium will take its place and its small moments will be no more. Nevertheless, while it continues to stand, there is a certain kind of time traveller who may appreciate the house as a film set, its history archetypal, signifying a life made simple by belonging to the privileged classes, but they will not escape how finite is imagination. That lice and termites feasted on its woods will not deter these nostalgic souls from guessing the rare moods of those who lived in it as if contentedly. They will finger the loop hooked through twisted wire serving as a gate latch, amble down the grassy drive to pause and breathe deeply under the old ansenna tree, hoping to catch an aroma of — they know not what. These dreamers will stir at the creaking joists crumbling under the weight of timbers settling further down on stumps, and they will swear they heard a thin tune, a snatch of song, that made the top branches of the old tree sigh. They will long to sit calmly in one of the rooms, leaning into cool breezes, listening, listening for rustling, some humming they believe to be echoes of times past. But they will not find photographs of the house at its best, when it was new and its garden was freshly planted and undergrown. When it is no longer there to see, they will see themselves. In their travel diaries, they will scribble vanities and aphorisms that amount to postscripts about where they have been and how well they have observed themselves there.

The amiable Patrick, living alone in an old bungalow on Jalan Dunn, liked to gather fellow Australians around him. Americans, too. According to Penang's social code, made more complex on the island by several distinctive races, these people of migrant nations complemented each other. They readily formed a sub-group within the broader classification of Europeans, distinct from the English whose language they shared.

Patrick's collection of backpackers and loquacious wayfarers were distinct, too, from the Australians across the channel at Butterworth. The type of people who came to him claimed to be right thinking, pacifists and post-modern solipsists. They had nothing to say to anyone working for a military outfit.

Patrick's employer, a Dutch firm of dredging engineers, had offered him a modern house in Taman Jesselton where most of the foreign business community clustered. This quiet leafy area, known as the Civil Lines on Jesselton Street in 1972, was, in 1982, known by its Malay name, its housing designs suburban in the European style.

Old houses crumbling under dense shade may not be part of the mental furniture of a Northern European businessman from a *slaapstadt*, a dormitory town. Or, as the grafitti artists of Patrick's boss's home town scrawl on bus shelters and on the walls of pedestrian underpasses, *drankstadt*, a town for agoraphobics and alcoholics. For Joop Waterend something clean with unchipped painted surfaces and no mildew could not be compared with an old British residence slumping on its stumps under the sunless canopy of a giant ansenna tree. Patrick insisted, widening his eyes in mock disbelief and playing an ironic grin round his mouth, "I've found a pure piece of history! 'T'll be like living in a movie! I'd like that!"

Minheer Waterend was surprised to meet an engineer, least of all an Australian, with a bent for history.

Patrick, a young man with 'fire in his belly', appealed to the blustering Waterend. He instructed the housing officer to satisfy the fantasies this *jonge* harboured. When he discovered a whole family of Indians came with the house, he laughed at the problem Patrick had landed himself with.

Wang Shi-zheng, the Dutch company's real estate broker, said, "They'll do any work you can give them. Clean. Cook. Garden. Wash. Can do all." He explained that the family had lived in the pavilion as the servants for the residents of the main house before the Second World War. They disappeared some time during the Occupation, probably to the mainland. Afterwards, they came back to resume their life in the pavilion as if they believed they were servants for the house even when it was empty.

Patrick discovered the family was more than he bargained for. His relationship with them was feudal, and his Australian life gave him nothing from which to learn his role. He may have been too generous. He gave money for a daughter's menarche, even though he was not too sure why that sort of thing was celebrated at all. He helped provide for a glittering prize presented to a young couple after the birth of a first son. He organised health care and intervened in police matters. He tried to ensure education was taken seriously and that the girls, most especially the girls, learnt an employable skill of some kind. The girls giggled when he installed a sewing machine in their quarters, but they dutifully went to the dress-making classes he paid for.

The mother of this seemingly endless family was his housekeeper. Meena occasionally skimmed off a bit of grocery money to make an offering to Sri Ganes, thanking the God of Good Luck for sending Tuan Patrick to rent the big house. After sprinkling holy water over her floral offerings to the deity, she cooked Tuan Patrick a special curry lunch. Tuan Patrick ate with relish, but he insisted on eating it with the family. The children squirmed and giggled when he sat on the floor with them. They stifled guffaws at his big blunt fingers burrowing into the rice and curry sauce. He was not as deft as they were.

To a sociologist, Tuan Patrick is a neo-colonial. To a strikingly poor family maximising good fortune perhaps opportunistically, this magnanimous young man happened to be in the house on Jalan Dunn at the express will of Sri Ganes who blessed their karma favourably. With the appearance of great sagacity, the adults nodded their heads and rolled their eyes, trusting their luck to hold good.

For the house was said to be haunted by a restless spirit.

When pressed, Meena widened her eyes dramatically. She neither wanted to scare Patrick away, nor wished to underplay a good story by too much caution. "My mother," she said, "say ghost lady wait for China Man!"

Her voice, grating the air, rose with the story. "She was his woman! Young Missee of this house, before the war. Yes, Tuan, you see her at the window sometime. In the evening. Dissember. Always Dissember."

He wished she would stop calling him Tuan! Urged her to tell him more. And he thanked Minheer Waterend for finding him a pure piece of history with a real history, "Complete with a ghost story."

Patrick winked a wry grin.

The Dutchman was not impressed. "Dredging. Patrick. Let us get on with the dredging! You'll find in these parts the labourers make excuses for not working. The excuse they like to make, always, is … a ghost."

But Patrick asked the labourers about a ghostly woman who smiled at the fishermen from their nets. He explained to them that he had heard other stories about her wallowing, when the tide was low, behind a cage of roots in the bay the company dredged. The labourers, surprised one of the bosses asked about these sightings, studied his face carefully to be sure that he listened. Then they drew quickly on their cigarettes. Through a veil of smoke, they added there was music too, the drawn-out note of a saxophone.

Patrick remained sceptical, quietly classifying these sightings as hallucinatory. He was certain the heat of the day bent rays to fracture shadows playing through light. He also held a vaguely formed impression that ghostly women often visit the sick to beckon them across the winkless body of water separating life from death. From Camelot to Ecuador, Death and its attendant ghosts have haunted the human consciousness in a remarkably similar way. They hover at the edges of the collective imagination, gesturing and whispering warnings like Hamlet's father and Banquo, or seething with preternatural eroticism like Catherine and Heathcliff. Before exhausted eyes waking within the febrile sleep of malaria or dengue fever, a lady's arm may rise out of a lake to the eerie sound of a horn. Human imagination, Patrick believed, was both borderless and finite, a mirror of the universe.

Patrick realised he superimposed his parents' house, a bungalow at Pennant Hills, a suburb of Sydney, Australia, on this one he found dwarfed under giant trees at the end of a long drive in Georgetown, known as Pinang of Penang Island, Malaysia.

His Georgetown house was not as large as it looked. Utility rooms, store room after galley, wash room after drying room, extended in a straight line from the back of the large front room, a place for receiving guests. A bathroom adjacent to this reception room crumbled in disrepair, a thick, rusted stain scoring a once white wash basin, the maroon and blue and white tiles cracked.

Behind a door scraping over the tiles, an old bedroom sloped headily downwards. Electric wires looped round the light socket at the centre of its ceiling, which was most probably originally decorated with plaster roses and a fine glass shade.

This house was debris. That was his lover, Gillian's, joke about it. It was, she said, an historical artefact, not knowing it shared an ambience with his parents' house where shadows lunged round doorways and thickened down a long central hallway. The pitched roof sloped low over deep verandahs and shielded the windows, just as the Penang house concealed its windows under deep eaves. He did not like the inside of the Sydney house. It was cold, and in winter he shivered over radiators. But the house surrounded its eyelessness with wild gardens distinguished by old scented roses, irises and camellias under towering if not stately eucalyptus trees. Patrick liked the scents from the garden. And he loved the comforting sound of the verandah boards' slow creaking in the mid-afternoon when he dragged his feet through grasses to the tennis court at the back.

Dreams and imagination roll with memories to make a composite reality some may dismiss as fanciful, even lacking in veracity. Gillian, an historian, may scoff, but for Patrick, both of the houses hinted at or evoked (he could not decide) the pleasure of slow living. Languor. He, in this house on Jalan Dunn, relished languor.

In the days of horses and carriages, people had the time to have a little chat when they passed on the street. Patrick liked that image. He pictured women dressed impeccably, twirling parasols to shade faces shadowed by impossibly large and veiled hats. The older ones would stiffly exchange words of greeting with the chief engineer — Patrick imagined he would have been the chief engineer — and the gentleman would have a chance to catch a glimpse of a shy daughter bowing her head slightly. He would have the time to admire the curve of a full, smiling mouth.

Whether out of respect for a feminist nicety or from her commitment to the history of the buildings more ordinary thus unromantic people worked in, Gillian could not resist puncturing Patrick's fanciful mirage. "Ghastly gossips! Patrick! Can't you imagine how closely everyone would've watched everyone?" And she went on as if wagging her finger at him, instructing him not to trust "An illusory elegance. And you're not to suffer it!" She laughed at his conjuring of quiet grace, and loved him with irritation for being a dredging engineer with a tendency for idiot fantasies.

Patrick asked for a good reason why he should abandon his dreams. He acknowledged they were derived more from the movies than from anything else he may have known. "I like it! It's a picture of grace." And his picture lingered, this time with him tipping his hat at a frilled parasol shielding half a pretty smiling face. "Nice'n slow," he said. Then, looking at Gillian as she settled down on floor cushions, he repeated, "You know. Nice'n slow."

The flat of his hand sliding through air extended the slowness.

It has to be said the drive off Jalan Dunn was designed for the slow pace of a horse and trap. Looking down its length towards the street, Patrick anticipated groups of people in long and voluminous white and cream clothes wending their way over its roughness, stepping fastidiously over the tyre tracks and the column of feathery grass growing down its centre. He caught himself smiling at his own embarrassment for standing there when he could not remember getting up from the spreadsheets he was studying or from the novel that he thought had engrossed him.

If waxy limbs ribboned the black night, arms and legs looping the gate, jiggling its awkward wiry latch, he held his breath. For an instant. Waiting. To hear voices chuckling, to see bodies standing under his porch light, a poor thing, better at obliterating than shafting light through the dead insects massing at the bottom of its concave fitting. Sometimes he ushered in a stray Australian in search of a shower and a bed, an anxious compatriot's face relieving him of his. On those occasions, he felt blood flow as if released from a knot high in his head. Other times, a group he forgot he had invited over for an after-dinner drink and chat would wander in to take over his front room. A quiet slow evening reading, perhaps being alone with Gillian, was doomed.

However, and not too many years after the house was built, an automobile had nosed through the gate. Patrick imagined the black box on wheels gently groaning as it rose and fell over the grassy driveway. And perhaps Patrick was right when he declared the automobile connived to preserve an appearance of respectability when inside its enclosure and travelling at a compelling speed, it concealed the disordering elements aiding and abetting ... he said democracy.

Certainly, the Missee of this house on Dunn Street, as it was before the Second World War, put to good use the chief engineer's, her Uncle Cedric's, Hillman Minx. In other words, a Hillman Minx chuffed merrily into the face of languor to effect revolutionary change.

Little did Patrick know how right Gillian was about the great lengths some people of the past went to protect themselves from recognition, greetings, questions — agreeable chat! How could he when his mental baggage was stuffed full of iconography remembered from the cinema? Forms and colours attaching themselves to heads angled more precisely than ever they could be in real life, responsive to music and lighting, intersected Patrick's final belief in all that was around him.

Film-makers may have conceived women like Willoughby's niece, Rose, a girlish young woman who may have studied the movements of Scarlet O'Hara in *Gone With the Wind*, or the gently pouting Dorothy Lamour dancing round the pillars of many an improbable tropical location, as a feminine effect, thus politicising people who were never involved in public life. By being a concept of feminine gesture and eye movement, that studied surprise flashed up on a screen and high above the more ordinary routine most of us accept as the reality of our daily lives, Rose and her ilk become, in the language of the trade, stars, constellations, larger and more dominating than observers who watch her story and fall in love with the effect of politicised femininity.

Meena and her family understand Rose without any cinematic instruction. As do the fishermen and the labourers who live in fear of the evening tide washing the shores of Penang Island. For them, she is a restless soul searching for her lover. She haunts the edges of their lives where the shadow of the sun cools and dreams invade, stunning their backbones with mortifying terror.

Yet Rose, in her real life, was less an effect than she was effective.

During the early months of 1941, she developed a habit of driving her uncle's Hillman Minx to a discreet parking spot in or near Penang Road. Then she took a rickshaw to another part of the town where, after inspecting the wares of a specialist shop for a decent interval, she took another rickshaw up Love Lane into Farquhar Street and to the E & O. It did not take long for some gossips to notice. They discussed 'that dreadful girl and her peculiar activities' in a highly speculative manner.

On other occasions, Rose waited for that sleepy hour after lunch when the clandestine lovers of Penang dashed like quick shadows across Georgetown. However she managed it, Rose perfected many complicated ways to meet her young man in the hotel room above the hibiscus garden and the vast glitter of the Indian Ocean.

Li-tsieng first saw Rose early in 1940 when he and one of his brothers and an uncle accompanied two of his older aunts and his younger sister, Chin-pei, to the Norwegian consulate where they were to be guests at afternoon tea. Rose startled him. Was it the silken hair? There was a stillness, a melancholy expression, and a slow, wide smile. Whatever attracted him, she was one among a bevy of young women invited to make this afternoon tea an event the Chinese guests of the Norwegians could not fault. Only the younger unmarried Wang girls were allowed to go beyond the precincts of the Wang family mansion with their almost elderly aunts. Li-tsieng's very young wife never left the mansion to attend these afternoon teas.

Li-tsieng's father invested a lot of money in the education of his children. Li-tsieng spoke German and English. Chin-pei was sixteen when the European women found her fluency in French and English 'most charming', and they hoped she would not be married too soon. They enjoyed her company, and agreed among themselves that she was 'enchanting, darling, if not altogether lively'.

That evening, Li-tsieng asked Chin-pei an abrupt question about the European women. He did not repeat his questioning, knowing the lattice behind which his own people screened themselves against a hostile world was tangled with quick judgements, vengeful conspiracies and brutal condemnations. He ascertained enough to establish a name and where the bearer of that name fitted into Georgetown society. That she was a senior engineer's niece, and the name of her uncle's employing firm, were the clues he needed to know.

How can we imagine the level of intrigue necessary for a young Chinese man to meet an English girl on an island under British rule during those last years of the Empire? The ladders bridging the Chinese and the European races were respectfully distanced before the Second World War. Flanked by several uncles and brothers, the young man's movements would have been, of necessity, deft.

Both the de-luxe hotels of Georgetown, the Runnymede and the E & O, held dinner dances and balls to celebrate important events like the birthday of one considered to be a dignitary, perhaps several years at the Bar, or distinguished services to property and the enactment of the law. These were occasions men of an eminent Straits Chinese family may have been invited to.

Would they have been invited to a girl's twenty-first? Unlikely. And Li-tsieng would not have been able to waltz. He would have been too nervous to hold a woman close to his body in public.

With the help of the movies and the way they magnify through simplification a constructed history, a frame squares with the Ink Spots jazzing up a meeting under a sky full of moons and stars. That band may well have passed through

Penang to play in the coconut grove at the Runnymede or on the lawn of the E & O. Their melodies sugared the dance floors of the 40s, their lyrics fascinated the kind of trysts loved by amateur romantics.

At a ball, a saxophonist escaping the madness let loose on Austrian streets, was amazed to notice a Chinese boy's eyes skim across the face of a young English woman. As his saxophone lowered, his curiosity directed him to watch carefully when an attendant brushed the young woman's arm. His heart warming for the love of an intrigue, the Austrian observed how the young woman blushed before she left the room. Perhaps his own experience taught him to guess she had a note to read. Within the traced arcs of his saxophone, he definitely caught a glimpse of that Chinese boy's eyes brightening a fraction when she sat at her table again. The saxophonist gauged with a pleasure reserved for the lovelorn how glazed were her eyes, how heavy were her limbs.

If she had caught sight of Li-tsieng, he would have stiffened. He would not have bargained for a direct and very public exchange even if it were only eye contact. But she too may have observed a code of etiquette unknown to cinemagoers and historians watching and reading about these events fifty years after they occurred. He, averting his eyes, may have caught a hint of a smile, enough for him to cherish the hope that a more substantial meeting was possible. He may have taken courage, too, in a kind of feminine delicacy we no longer bother ourselves with.

In any event, conspiring to meet Rose privately required an astute sense of play. And he was a spoilt man, Li-tsieng. He would have his way.

Perhaps one auspicious evening when he arranged for a note to find its way into Rose's hands, Li-tsieng, looking sharp and waiting for her reaction, saw her eyes rested on a curtained doorway, suggesting to him and watching for him to back out of the room. The saxophonist, sweating at the boom microphone and familiar with their hesitancies, pressed the blower firmly to his lips. His playing more vigorous, he distracted the dancers to an energetic spin so that Rose could slip unnoticed through the veil of curtains out to the moonlit night.

It was a brief meeting, that first one, of fingers sliding along the parapet. Another note, a flicker of the eyes, a sigh, lost to the sea's ceaselessness.

What could Rose have been thinking?

The following afternoon she suddenly felt herself to be inadequately dressed in an unsophisticated pale blue voile. Florally sprigged, it was a girl's dress, not the daring gown to wear when tottering on the brink of a grand passion in a room filled with yellow rose buds.

At first, Li-tsieng was so overcome by the audacity of his success in having the niece of a senior engineer of a respected firm agree to an assignation, he turned his head away. She stared directly at him, expectantly. His embrace was therefore a bit rough. More the stallion, she may have observed if she had lived to tell her own story, than a distinguished lover. But Rose did not second guess her stallion. When she lay in the circle of his pale, hairless arms, more excited than spent, giggling softly at the single fold of his eyelid, she was pleased by a sense of voluptuous power she recognised as her own, and she wanted that power to stay with her forever. Rose was canny enough to want adventure.

Nothing happened at Pennant Hills to prepare Patrick to understand tragedy. None of the movies he liked to see adequately evoked the foreboding of a mid-afternoon in 1941 when the saxophonist released long practice notes into the pearling light.

The Austrian's blue eyes, resting on the mirroring of sea by sky, glided over the lustre to the house on a back street in Vienna he hastily left a night or two before the Anschluss.

Pressing the horn, he blew perfectly pitched notes to relieve grief's hurt for the politically active girlfriend he abandoned to the sadism of the Nazis. His mouth twisted. A note curled. An awkward crotchet splattered and failed to rise. His body, stinking of whisky and Sumatran tobacco, sweated out his numb act called life.

Blowing steadily, he scored a melancholy bar across the Straits. He instructed his body to overcome disgust, pack a suitcase and move on. Survive! Perhaps his understanding of the news as it was reeled in the local cinemas by courtesy of Gaumont British News, and his reading between the lines of bombast printed in *The Straits Echo* and *The Singapore Herald*, informed him as the months sped by that future events on the dreamy Pearl of the Orient would be dire. Music, and he lowered his horn to stare at the mesmerising light that made his eyes tear, filled its sweet note into the voided heart.

Rose disturbed his contemptuous self. Like a soft breathing, she slipped through the shrubbery near his window. He wiped his eye, he winced, and she was gone. The place where he had seen her, by a mauve hibiscus, widened. It seemed to smile. And he smiled, for the goodness lovers dispel.

When Gillian lies in Patrick's arms, he relates to her more and more details of Meena's extraordinary if fractured story about a young Englishwoman whose ghost hovers around the front windows for a few days every December. When the first reports of the Japanese landing at Kota Bharu came through, it seemed Rose's aunt and uncle were thrown into turmoil. Her uncle had booked a passage to Ceylon, but the departure date he chose was too late. Her aunt sat on trunks, drinking and crying while the servants packed away household effects.

Then Rose disappeared.

The servants knew where she had gone. At the wet market that fateful morning, hoisting a chicken by its legs, Meena's mother heard the gossip that a young Wang, dramatically in love, had left his wife with the rest of his family in Chile. The chauffeur heard at the petrol bowzer that 'a certain young chappie' was back at one of the mansions by the sea. Tight-lipped, the servants had no doubt Rose was with him.

According to Meena's story, Rose's aunt and uncle waited one long day for her. They left the night after the first bombing of the airfield. The aunt, soaked terribly in perfume and smelling of gin, her cream travelling dress already crumpled and stained, sat high on her baggage, her painted mouth grinning, her eyes streaming tears for fear and for Rose. She moaned and sang and she kicked her feet until a lorry from her husband's firm parked under the front windows. Several men threw her baggage up and hoisted her into the cabin where she sat mute between the driver and the chief engineer, a child clenching a soiled lace handkerchief in her fist.

Then, Meena's story goes, Rose came back. She wandered from shambled room to shambled room, playing records, singing snatches of song, refusing to speak to anyone. Rummaging for clothes in a trunk left for her, she threw on dresses and hats and discarded them while tugging at the curtains in the front room.

Patrick, explaining to Gillian that Meena's grasp of time was always hazy, adduces she came back on the evening of the ninth, not leaving the house again until the afternoon of the tenth.

Wanting the story to be whole, Gillian makes him go over the details of time again and again. Together they speculate. Perhaps she expected to sail to Ceylon with her aunt and uncle after all; perhaps she expected to argue her reasons for staying. But Meena was adamant. Her mother said the young Missee appeared one evening, made a mess with all her clothes and things, tugged at the curtains in the front room then, in the afternoon of the following day when the light was going all pearly, she rushed under the branches of the big tree. And that was the last Meena's mother saw of the young Missee.

Patrick, touching Gillian's cheek lightly, brings Meena's story to a close. Despite suspending belief, he draws her to him. He hears a rippling as if his telling unsettles a troubled spirit. He is certain then that the house subsides into a sadness it never quite expelled from its walls.

♓

7. a spirit wanders

There, in the house, condensing into the walls, is the spiritual essence of a troubled being. Shadows cool the corridor. Rooms gently rot. Window frames sink around the glass, cracking some. A smell of mildewed dust bothers the air. The sagging floorboards and the rust staining the wash basins are facts Patrick lives with. No gloom pleats into the shadows where curtains draped forty years before his time. But when Jacqui Dark stood under the ansenna tree, light bent to give depth to the restlessness seeking an escape. Gillian thought she saw it, too, an incandescence. And the hairs on her arms stood up, painfully frozen from a cold that was of another world.

A spirit wanders.

At night, Meena struggles to put her children to bed. They sleep with their arms wound round each other's necks. They are darkly beautiful, their eyelids like honeyed snails, their lips unfurling fronds. But in the small hours of the morning, Meena hears a shriek. She looks up from her bed to see one wild arm thrash the mat, one thrusting knee pierce the night. White teeth gnash. Quickly she slides from her husband's side to lift from the twist of arms one of her brood. She cradles the thin body, and lilts a nightsong.

Meena, in her heart, knows the spirit sighs when she hears her singing the old lament. After all, she reasons, this is a ghost of a young woman who has lost the man she may have been destined to partner. Meena does not know it but her instinct tells her these ghosts, all around the world, wander sadly, sometimes through snow storms, sometimes when fog thickens on a moor, sometimes where wind whips across sea smashing rocks. They search, these ghosts, restlessly, savagely, for their lovers. They do not inhabit a dank room to weep soggy tears.

Her singing quietens the child in her arms.

By the window the spirit wanders. The spirit searches for her lover.

It is conceivable that Jacqui Dark may like the story about a girl called Rose waiting for her boyfriend to send her a message, a story that ends in both their deaths. Even though she likes to live in the evolving present without any equivocation, Jacq is not without heart. She likes movies about ghosts seeking to reconcile unfinished love affairs, old Black & Whites screened late at night. She would rather watch them than find herself weeping at televised dramas about a whole range of maudlin attachments. The old love stories conveyed to Jacq the human capacity for loyalty.

In the way Jacqueline sees the world, wandering down and round the curvilinear latitudes and longitudes searching for patterns of light, it is an act of awful resignation to spend time seated on a sofa, walking round a room, running fingers over silver ashtrays, opening and shutting a cigarette box lying under a table lamp, waiting firstly for the hour to leave on an assignation, then for a note. Jacqui, who may be bruised by a failed love affair, is sexually pragmatic.

Haunted by an inexplicable sadness, she is, some would say, attractive to men, displaying a seductive quality, allowing her right hand to drift between her mouth and the other's eyes, more or less hypnotising with gestures rather than bothering with conversation. Jacqui never confuses the signals. Sexual attraction is not the same thing as loving someone.

Floating, drifting through many places, her maps chart her trackings from casual lover to casual lover. Some lovers want to reassure her, to explain to her that her habit of graduating from bed to bed is not good for her. Most, however, find sealed inside her thin skin the obduracy of a tough survivor accommodated to the moment.

There she is in Jakarta not several days after staying with Patrick. Jacq presses her fingers into a mound of rice. The only other customer in the nasi Padang restaurant shoves at rice and chillied eggs with a spoon and fork. Jacq likes the man's striped jacket. She is deaf to his loud complaining. Through a mouthful of food, he declares that the place's a hole. "Everything in it's shitty! Shit! Shit! Shit!"

He shouts, "Shouldn't eat here! Flies've crawled all over the stuff in that window!" As an afterthought, he introduces himself.

"Bill. Berringen."

"Brisbane."

Jacq smiles.

Then she trails beside Bill, passing a group of skylarking boys who pull out fluoro combs to slick through their stylishly leonine hair. They swap a lewd joke at Bill's expense. When he whips round, his face florid, his tongue lashing at their rudeness, they laugh, partly surprised that he understands their local dialect, the bawdy Betawee of Jakarta. They congratulate themselves for finding the mark in this Johnny from Australia who picked up the woman they had seen wandering into the nasi Padang restaurant. She does not understand the joke. Nor does she care much for Bill's spluttering rage. Nevertheless, she leaps into the cabin of his jeep and looks at him sidelong when he throws the gear stick. For his part, he senses a curling of shoulders and a melting as if she is working towards a seductive moment. He talks all the time he manoeuvres the jeep through the slow weaving of cars and buses and bicycles criss-crossing in front and around them.

Bill.

Berringen.

Brisbane.

Nice enough. And there. In the flesh. Flesh to touch.

She will drift in the climate of his bed later in the day, perhaps late in the night.

And what of Gillian?

Contradiction does not arrest her.

She hates any blood rushing, heart pumping, knees weakening. She fears the sensation, the hot pain. That her whole body in its tumult denies its excess is an excess itself works against her. By controlling the terrible strength of her physical responses, which mix horribly with memories of unwanted gropings, Gillian will never let herself explore the borders of her humanity.

In a conventional narrative set in those decades of the twentieth century described as the second wave of feminism, Gillian Hindmarsh would have been cast as a realist. She may be a character not given so much to wistful yearnings or surreal psycho-dramas as to plotting a path from birth to death with an eye firmly fixed on personal development. For the greater part of her life, she may be described as attractive, that is to say not beautiful, but adept with accessories to highlight her better features whether or not she believed them to complement her colouring. She understood she was fortunate to have good hair, and that she was blessed with lovely eyes. But Gillian was marred by a quick, sometimes brusque, manner. She was impatient. In this, her appearance and her manner did not properly fit with that of the historian.

In photographs stored in Kodak envelopes or filed in the plastic pockets provided by modern albums, an unnamed figure will doubtless face her observers. They will comment on and laugh at her knees that bulged from beneath extremely short mini-skirts. In those days, her hair straggled over the shoulders of cheap Indian printed garments. Revealed from beneath these long flowing gowns, an anklet of bells and charms caught the sun and glinted, blurring her photograph at the bottom, far right-hand corner. An older self adapted to the routine of skirts and tops will lean over someone's shoulder to stab a finger at herself self-consciously sporting a matador suit and flounced blouse. Both these Gillians, although no prisoner of fashion, may be imprisoned by a style that described her as conventional, middle-class, suburban.

Gillian's story may be compelling. It may be implausible, but it is not bewitching. Her journey from farmer's daughter to scholarly historian admits no controversy. Gillian is one of those nice girls who, in the early 1960's, were beginning to leave places like Newrybar to attend the Teachers' College in the mountains where she studied infants' and primary school teaching. At the College, she had a good time, meaning she was popular with the boys and not too serious about her studies. But disenchantment with teaching quickly set in. Desperately, she read Arts, firstly be correspondence and then by attending the University in Sydney. She had to escape standing at the head of a classroom.

Footnoted in someone else's story or firmly fixed in her own, her character, persistent, some would say dogged, is not usual for enchantment. She is not charming.

Gillian's tenacity surprised herself.

When she was ranked among the primary school teachers of New South Wales, Gillian discovered the awfulness of not belonging to the group. In the small community of her first posting, she was alone, simultaneously scorned by the adults for coming in from the outside, stonewalled by their dull children, and despised by the young men for being young and single and educated and a woman.

Watching her younger sister's transformation at University from gauche child to resolute individual, Gillian analysed the predicament she found herself in. Without begging the question, she sought opportunities to manipulate in order to circumvent a life stalemated before it had really begun.

After successfully completing one year of a Bachelor of

Arts degree by correspondence, Gillian judged her chances well when she appealed to a new inspector for a transfer to a Sydney school. An accidental meeting in an inner-city pub led her to inquire about the courses offered by the University of Sydney's Department of Indonesian and Malayan Studies. A love affair encouraged her to read History. She began a Masters' degree in Colonial architectures. She later concentrated her study, narrowing it down to examine the historical influences on modern Malaysian public buildings, thus upgrading to PhD status.

Gillian's long education may not ensure her an economically advantaged future. Rather, and Gillian knew this, it was a simple insurance against ever having to experience again the hostility of indifference.

On any evening in December 1982, when her exhaustion after reading insect scratched bureaucratic documents all day burrows through her whole being, Gillian may be found sitting in her bed at Island Glades, a suburb adjacent to the Universiti Sains Malaysia, Pulau Penang. She reads the local newspaper called *The Star*.

She is obsessed by a story about a family who did not honour the letter of their mother's last will and testament. Without bothering to acknowledge their mother's wishes, the sons proceeded to sell the old family house. They wanted capital to invest in their expanding business. The old mother wanted her eldest brother, a widower, to live in the house until he died. But the men of the family fixed a FOR SALE to the house, and advertised the house in *The Star*. According to the police report, after the steps were taken, the house was mysteriously bombarded by rocks at eight o'clock precisely every night for one week. Rocks flew as if from nowhere. It was not until the thing was sorted out with the house being kept in the family the way the dead one wanted it that the rocks stopped flying.

Gillian loves these stories of preternatural occurences. She feasts on intrigues complete with apparitions and other ghostly sightings. She likes reminding Patrick these reports printed in newspapers made history a more than curious narrative. The irrational logic of them balances a brain plodding through the research required for a thesis, she told Patrick. "It's the solemn recording of the inexplicable I find refreshingly human."

"Mills and Boon," she says to Patrick with disarming honesty. "All that cheap romantic stuff is not far from where I am."

He was then uncertain this was a confession of a weakness in her overall intellectuality, or an excuse to explain her apparent poor taste in newspapers.

Gillian read the tabloids and the women's magazines, the ones filled with reports about sexual liaisons and scandalous movie stars. Adrift with these starry-eyed beauties, she indulged a sort of romance she loved in old movies. "Bee 'n' double U, Patrick. The big Black And Whites. With blue moons and crossed stars."

After she finishes reading on any of those evenings, she folds her newspaper and puts it aside, and lifts the portrait of the young woman she has stolen from the archive. A slight pout rounds out the woman's lips. A shadow falls from her waist to her backbone where the cloth of her dress folds. Her eyelids are heavy. Gillian, running a thin fingernail over the surface of the photograph, recalls the nutty smell of Patrick's pale yellow freckled skin.

She puts the portrait on her bedside table, and snuggles into her pillow.

Sleep comes in swiftly with the morning vision of Mr Mukhapadai standing in the doorway, offering her tea and smiling through streams of sunshine. She swims upwards into the whorls of those smiles.

Would Gillian admit the spirit, have it swim a story through her?

Rose was not so equivocal.

In a cool room, her arms above her head for a dress fitting, Rose was more down to earth than Gillian. Although a melancholy deepened the colour of her cornflower blue eyes, she was not as passive to life's circumstance as is Jacq. But her space for making decisions was more constrained than it was for either Jacq or Gillian. Her future, she knew, was with a man. Not any man, but one for whom she professed a love, and he would become her husband to whom she would devote her life. Her whole life depended on her success in matrimony. The alternative, to become a call girl, was not part of her understanding of the world.

She needed, of necessity, to exercise a certain caution.

Rose was involved in tennis tournaments and the women's pages.

Li-tsieng was her lover, the moon over the water was 'simply marvellous' and Jean Littlejohn Aarberg's advices on how to host a successful dinner party were 'quite pedestrian, don't you think, Aunt?'

Aunt Margaret, reclining on a sofa in the reception room, agreed. "Darling! One becomes So Hot. Really. Dinner parties are not so much Fun. Do you really Think," she said, running her finger down a column in the *Singapore Herald*. "Do you *really* think Peaked Pink Butterfly-winged Napkins would make a dinner party a success?"

Rose's Aunt Margaret ashed her cigarette in a tiny copper and silver inlaid brass dish set under a gold tasselled lampshade. Two white porcelain elephants guarded the front door. Her floors were covered with Indian rugs. On her walls hung a collection of Iban weaponry Cedric had acquired, at odds with some small watercolours of tropical scenes she had executed and an oil of a sunset with palm trees by a less competent, more dramatic artist.

Arranged on a nesting of three elaborately carved teak

side-tables were portraits of 'the family back home'. When Aunt Margaret was alone and she had drunk far too much, she would pick up these silver framed portraits, her cheeks awash with silent tears. Margaret missed the quiet gathering together at the fireside in winter when, hugging knees and staring at the flames, glass in hand and with little to say, she would pass an uneventful and cosy evening with her brothers and her sister. She missed the bedtime suppers of sweet spicy breads and tea. She missed the smells of spring and autumn, the changing seasons, the softer colours and the seductive perfumes of flowers. She missed the low crack of the ball on the bat on a moist green lawn when a spring game of cricket was played.

Margaret Vane had married down, her family having no other engineers in its ranks, nor any direct contact with coolies slushing in mire to dig and wash for tin, which her husband described as one among his 'professional activities'. Cedric Willoughby, a soft-hearted chap, was bearable only because his family were well-to-do, therefore able to camouflage the fact that his father's wealth was self-made. Colonially acquired.

Margaret did not regret Cedric, she loved his ditheriness. But no matter how hard she tried, she missed the complacencies that made the predictable life of Kent amiable.

In Penang, Margaret Willoughby spent her days supervising the shopping and the preparation of food for the daily menus, planning a flower garden and watching over the gardener to ensure water was not spared and the soil was properly tilled. She directed the housemaid to air the linen and clothing (mildew was a problem), and instructed the *dhobi* on the mysteries of washing and pressing her best embroidered table cloth. She ordered the chauffeur to keep the Hillman well-oiled, and asked the tailor to take Cedric's measurements for a dozen shirts. "The War," she breathed with incredulity, "has interrupted his London order." And Margaret spent hours dressing to attend functions.

When she met a desultory trio for bridge, she always wore lace mittens, a lace handkerchief tucked between two wrist buttons, and her frock was usually a light georgette. The social pages often carried her picture, apparently joyful in the company of the town's municipal fathers at a garden party. Margaret caused a stir at an afternoon tea under a marquee arranged to welcome the young debutante who was the bride of Governor Shenton Thomas.

Memorably elegant in wide picture hats and tailored linen, she was a conversation piece before, during, and after, the Spring and Autumn meets at the Penang Turf Club. She silenced the gathering in the members' half of the small grandstand, the part reserved for white people and the wealthy whose colour was made unimportant by their ownership of horses. She looked lovely in a straight-skirted grey grosgrain silk with wide white epaulettes. It was pinned between the breasts with a white kid camellia, a design that later decades adapted to cheaper fabrics. Before the outbreak of hostilities, her sister shopped for her in Paris. The War, according to Margaret, was a nuisance to her, diminishing as it did the choices her wardrobe offered.

The local chatterboxes saw her fastidiousness as 'irresponsible'. Clearly she was not the sort of woman who should have in her charge a young woman of marriageable age — a young woman who, 'by all reports', had been seen walking down the corridor away from the powder room at the E & O at unusual times of the day.

My goodness!

At the Penang Turf Club, at the meet that no one knew was to be the last for several years, those with hawk eyes and a ready tongue watched Mrs Willoughby, stylish in white, and Willoughby's niece. The younger woman wore something lemony. With cream, it was said, and her small hat was veiled. A murmur of approval passed round some of the women standing in the grandstand. A waspish pair watched to see how 'the little mischief' connived to send a young man discreet signals by playing a finger game with her gloves.

Rose left on some people an indelible impression.

As for Aunt Margaret, she was better remembered for her dress than for herself. Even better than for her drinking problem. She smiled blissfully, the reason for her happiness hinted at but not pursued by those who 'never miss a trick', their suggestions, generally speaking, not canvassed as fact.

If there was an historical record of these smallnesses of life, it would show that Rose at the last Gold Cup meeting before the Occupation watched a young man threading his way through the crowd milling at the fence. At a given signal — on this occasion he raised his Panama — she whispered to her aunt that she felt hot and dusty and ... "Headachy, Aunt Margaret. Meet you at home." And before the dear aunt could protest, the 'slip of a thing' had vanished.

Rose wove her way through the crowd of men crushing the bookies' stands and, on the toes of her cream buckled shoes, her clutch bag held at an angle to shield her face, she slipped between the horses circling under the tree outside the stables.

One of the Boyanese strappers, a young member of a group of families employed by the Turf Club to care for the horses, frowned mightily at the woman swiftly circling through the horses. He saw some army boys looking up and catching sight of her. Surprise interrupted those white men's hands running up and down the flank of a chestnut mare. But when they straightened to call out to the 'quite nice bit on the loose', she disappeared under the clock. The strapper frowned with disgust. He stared hard at the woman who, not belonging to anyone, put her head down and dashed through the gateway. Deeply offended, he spat his contempt.

A Rover was waiting at this side entrance. The gloved hands of a uniformed driver held its door open for her. Rose stepped into its leathery shadows where Li-tsieng sat comfortably. He smiled. "This is Uncle Cho's. The race track," Li-tsieng said to her, "will keep him busy for as long as we need to be together."

The E & O was almost empty of its staff.

The doorman paced the front steps. The kitchen staff was reduced to two. One receptionist dozed at the front desk. But just about everyone else was at the Turf Club for Gold Cup Day.

There was no Sikh band striking up a doleful note on the lawn under the palm trees. No crowd of uniformed men stood round in the bar, drinking to the cheers celebrating the football score. Nor were there any women walking to the powder room. No groups of women clustered in the main foyer to share a secret about a girl's glad eyes so clearly audible it went by the name of 'the whispering room'.

When the dance was on, these women gathered to sit on velvet covered chairs. Leaning across a table into their own reflections, they dabbed powder on their noses, rouged their cheeks and reddened their mouths. Those standing in front of the long mirror would adjust taffeta blouses and tug at tulle skirts. Perhaps a rare one paused to make a rosebud of her lips. Turning sideways to walk a step or two to admire the swing of a panelled skirt or the full swell of a wide gown inspired by Scarlet O'Hara acting out a love story in *Gone with the Wind*, this one would sigh for the film screening in Singapore and coming to Penang. It was a favourite, much written about in the newspapers.

Satisfied with her impression, this one would smile at herself, raise a shoulder slightly, then, swiftly, she took the door.

All of these people were at the race track.

But for the Austrian.

The saxophonist packed his bag.

Waiting for the time of day when he would go down to

Swettenham Pier to embark his ship, he smoked his favourite Sumatran, a richly aromatic tobacco leaf rolled in fat cigars, and a good companion when taking in one last long look at the light changing from pearl to almond over the Straits. He was emptying his mind of memories, dwelling in the lighted moment, tensing another part of himself in preparation for arrival in Australia.

It was then laughter washed through him, and the light intensified. His thoughts buckled under the water mirroring the sky. He looked away for fear of being blinded.

Seated in a room, its door open, was the young woman whom he had watched for some months playing a game with shadows filtering through the hibiscus. Her lemon clad body leant back in a wicker chair. Laughing quietly, she was stroking ungloved fingertips over the cheek of her companion, a young man he recognised was Wang Li-tsieng. He was passing her a plate of pastries. Their being together like this without making love, simply sitting over tea, kindled a warmth that surprised them both, and she was adoring him.

Their attitude was relaxed. They had no need to hide. They believed everyone was at the Turf Club.

But for the Austrian.

But for the Austrian, striding through the foyer whose acoustics hid no secrets. He hailed a rickshaw. The violence of his heartbeat shook his rib cage. Bars of music ripped through his gut to commemorate yet another lovesick pair.

(When he blew a pure note above the sweating dancers in the country he chose to migrate to, the saxophonist wept for the unblemished love he had seen on his last afternoon in Penang, for the woman he left in Austria, for his fear of the jackboot ...,

And he hanged himself.)

Folding her child's long thin limbs across its waist, her head rolling from lack of sleep, Meena eases her body from sitting to lying on the floor where she heard the long sad note of a horn.

In Jakarta, Bill Berringen whistled in his sleep, twitched and bucked and shuddered dead still. Jacq's tired body did not welcome Bill's sweating back. She sat near the edge of his wet flesh in a room smelling of mangoes.

Nearer to breaking day, soft soundings muffled — stone on stone, wood clacking wood, cymbals rattling. Kitchen, animal, pious habits, who knows? A droning. A note dragging a voice. And a thousand imams chorused, their voices undulating, wavering, rippling the fungally apricot Jakarta air. Then a rooster crowed. Roosters crowed. Less than magically, cacophonous poultry closed over the last of the disharmonic recordings from the muezzin, the electronically transmitted summons for the faithful to pray.

In Penang, Gillian sits up, her hand clasped over her mouth, afraid the smooth-skinned young man, his hand curved like an unopened lotus by her hip, was not a dream.

♓

8. *a matter of identity*

On Swettenham Pier an impeccable young man stood in thin shade. He had bright eyes. One habitually glanced to his right, and the other took in the scene of his uncles, Cho and BK, overseeing blue-black Tamils and leathery Chinese straining the ropes. Uncle Cho commanded the coolies winching the family shrine, the Goddess of Mercy cushioned in black lacquered chests boxed in straw and timber shavings lining larger chests, into the hold of a steamship. A winch screeched through the yelling and grunting and groaning of the men. A horse, caged and waiting to be hoisted high then lowered to the ship's deck, kicked and neighed. It sweated fear. But wafts of discarded fish scales and rotting prawn shells, sump oil and petrol fumes overpowered the thick smell of the horse's fright.

    Uncle BK switched a cane behind his back, a sign he was having to control his impatience with the coolies. He cocked his shoe on its heel, to study the clean cuff of his cream trousers or the shining tip of his tanned leather shoe. He paused, twirling the cane. The young man guessed Uncle BK ground his teeth when he rocked on both heels. He knew, too, his uncle kept an eye out for him, Li-tsieng, the family fop who wore a yellow rosebud in his lapel, a peacock Uncle BK tried to prevent straying into a hussy's arms at any time of the day.

    Li-tsieng fingered his fob watch. He flicked open the case. His right eye read the time, the other continued to hold down the scene. The jerking of the minute hand interdicted the moment he saw a dexterous set of arms and legs attempt to spirit away an aunt's camphor wood chest. When his Uncle BK discovered the thieves, Li-tsieng's right eye measured the distance across the ropes and chains and winches and cranes, and his left eye saw a cane crack across a Tamil's back. Without hesitation, he walked behind cargo into a well of sunlight.

Uncle BK's bullying silenced the ropes. Three men cowered, and one other tried to melt among dumb-faced fellow workers who witnessed Uncle Cho magisterially sending for the port police to arrest the thieves.

No one saw Li-tsieng glance down Weld Quay past a bullock cart at a huddle of rickshaws. Most were pulled by a man between shafts. Only one was the new type powered by a man riding a three-wheeled cycle.

Li-tsieng signalled that one.

He walked into heatwaves that danced all around and over him. The driver pulled the hood of the small carriage up, and the body of his passenger vaporised when he rose through the crazed buckling of harsh light.

Only the quick would catch sight of him, Li-tsieng, a shadow sliding into a rickshaw.

He was his own invention. Wang Li-tsieng was no imitation of his uncles and his father.

Li-tsieng exuded a pervasive warmth when he settled in the rickshaw, gently bouncing with the rhythm of his transport. Not anticipating anything of the future beyond the next afternoon in 1941 when he will steam by ship away from Rose, Li-tsieng patted his tightening collar. Excitement focussed him and disappointment controlled his hands. He was comfortable, if not with his love life that the war promised to interrupt, at least with himself. The chap he sometimes saw reflected in mirrors was quietly confident and alert, a willowy figure in a quality suit.

Perhaps to satisfy a mild impatience with the speed of the rickshaw, Li-tsieng sometimes pressed a gloved finger against its pleated curtain. He heard the wheels of the cycle crunch a gravelled path, and he felt the vehicle draw to a halt. Quickly stepping down to the pavement, he tugged at his gloves. He faced the entrance hall of the E & O, the small de-luxe hotel Armenian brothers had built along the esplanade to display an ancient skill in creating beautiful things for the better purpose of selling pleasure.

Paying the driver and hurrying between potted palms and a gathering of soldiers, Li-tsieng avoided the lustrous eyes of a Sikh doorman whose wife had heard from a certain housekeeper of Dunn Street an English Missee conducted herself most strangely with a young man of a big Straits Chinese family.

Li-tsieng's footfall retreated up a small flight of stairs. He strode along a corridor open to the sea. The yellow sky arched over the Straits, but Li-tsieng had no eye for the mirrored plane of seasky, no nose for the salt spray. He fitted a key to a lock, pushed open a door, and snapped it shut behind him.

Did Li-tsieng rush to the edge of ecstasy?

Was he assured his confinement with the woman who waited for him near the hotel garden would not be disturbed? The historical record will not tell us. No document exists to enrich the annals, but love may thumb a story rivalling scenes of men more assertively masculine than Li-tsieng, of women more faintingly feminine than Rose, stories witnessed at the cinema in all of its innumerable fictions.

Dissipating energies and money on women in his search for an allusive something he witnessed at the movies helped him believe he was suave. But he was fearful his fervour denied him passion. Intuition cautioned him against haste. The rhythm of the man was not complacent. Li-tsieng was bundled zest, a quick eye watching the world above a fluid stride taking care not to break and run. He took time to understand affection, something the European novels he read denied the routine of marriage, which was for him arranged, a dull engagement with a fractious girl whose duty was to bear him a son.

So strangely Mandarin. As a Straits Chinese, indeed a Baba of Penang, his name should be Hokkien or Cantonese, less likely Hakka or Hainanese. Does this fishy tale protect his family's identity from too much easy speculation, they being of the elite, leaders in a community, a circumspect people well practised at concealment behind misleading disclaimers?

Whatever the ethnicity, the generation taking over after the Second World War took care not to be too foolhardy when picking through Western habits for new angles on old ideas. Like his father, Wang Shi-zheng enjoyed spending money, but in order to indulge the power of negotiating business deals and spending on building a new world. If it is proved that obsession shapes the destinies of both, may it also be that ethno-genetic racial type-casting steadies the pace that is leading Shi-zheng to raze old streets to make way for tower blocks?

And his father?

Li-tsieng rushed to his passionate love of Rose.

Li-tsieng liked the shy turn of her head. Her colours — pink skin, yellow hair, blue eyes. He liked her slow response, the back stepping, gaze direct, fixed on his eyes in a way he found offensive in his wife. He may have ordered champagne and a tray of *nyonya* pastries called top hats served with chilli sauce. But it's doubtful that he told her he was leaving the very next day on his father's instructions for Chile.

For this was an afternoon in September, 1941.

Not to be diverted from celebrating his farewell, Li-tsieng had the bellboy in his pay set up a camera and lamps. He urged Rose to pose for a session of photography, first leaving a trail of clothes to the bathroom where he sank her into a warm foaming water. That was where they ate the top hats, licking the spilled chilli sauce from each others' chins, washing the greasy pastry down with the champagne.

Li-tsieng was no weight lifter. He was not able to lift her

out of the bath. When she stood up, he wrapped her in a large towel and she patted herself dry. He passed over her head a costume he bought for her, a satin evening gown with straps as narrow as spaghetti straws descending from the nape of her neck to the low slung back at her waist. It slithered over her warm pink skin.

Spinning in her own magnificence, Rose arched her back. Her body ballooned, and Li-tsieng combed the curls waving across her forehead. But he was impatient. He ran across the room to disappear, a sinewy figure lost under black cloths to fiddle with lenses and lights. Rose waited for him to succeed focussing the lenses, framing the object of his desire that was herself. And running her hands up and down her thighs over the cool cloth draped over her nakedness, she ached erotically for him.

Rose sensed in Li-tsieng his urgency exceeding his usual demands. She believed the war made him intense as it had everyone else she knew. Khaki was filling the clubs and the hotels. She had no end of admiring young men to partner her on the dance floors and at the tennis club. Her uncle spent more time than was usual away from home. When he was there in Dunn Street, twiddling with the knobs of the wireless to hear the news broadcast, pointing the carving knife above the Sunday roast or bending over the cocktail cabinet, he was remote, withdrawn into worried silences. Her aunt drank more, waving the gin bottle openly at Rose after lunch, inviting her to join her before retiring for an afternoon sleep. "Darling!" she said with a hiccup. "A nip for a nap! It's so … Good. For One!" Neither aunt nor uncle actually spoke about the war. But at the tennis club, the other women agreed the war in China was four years long and it followed, surely, the Japanese had no capacity left to come further south? Surely!

Rose thought to ask Li-tsieng why he had a sudden interest in photography when a big vacancy inside her yawned. Guessing he was about to go away without leaving her an explanation, she smiled. Passive to her intuition, she curled her shoulders slightly to look at the solitary lens directed at her. The mechanical eye caught the light glancing off her tooth, catching too the low slant of her eyelid anticipating her soft moaning when Li-tsieng slid his hand under the heavy satin hem of her gown. She sighed for her mouth to crush his lips.

Such a love as this could have been tested for its rarity if those two had survived the war.

Light cascaded, light cascades, star points of light cascading, runnels spilling where there's the shape of a tail fin suggesting water.

Twenty years later, in 1961, a Vanguard cruises the same stretch of Weld Quay that Wang Li-tsieng jolted along on that day in 1941, seated in the back of a rickshaw. The son unknown to him, Wang Shi-zheng, elbows the sun burning the edge of the window on the driver's side of his car. He studies the line of buildings, the old godowns and outlets for stevedoring ropes and chains stringing the Quay where he envisages skyscrapers, shopping centres and a giant telecommunications tower.

He likes to sit in the quiet of the breakfast room of the E & O, a Tiger beer at his elbow when he shakes out *The Straits Times* and the local newspaper, *The Straits Echo*, to read about the new politics and to study the Classifieds for the right sale to pick up on or the best tender to subvert or compete for. He is patient. Lee Kwan Yew is impressive and yet to make the mark that Shi-zheng is predicting he will accomplish. Despite his youth, Shi-zheng is perceptive. He shrewdly guesses no one at the Turf Club is placing bets on how Penang politics, the rivalry between the City Council and the State Government, will prevent the Low Cost Housing Committee its successes.

Spellbound, and with no desire for desire like his father before him, Shi-zheng wants bricks and the smell of mortar.

After scribbling notes, suggestions for his uncles to vet, he wanders through the hotel and lingers along its corridors to lean on the parapet outside the room where his father dallied with Rose. Unlike his father, he gives himself the time to pause above the sheet of mirrored sky stretching across the Straits.

The sea's soft lap makes a sound that invades his pores, a gentleness that bumps under a broken tile. The light pearls. A cool breeze brushing his forehead feels like a cool hand passing over his brow. Flowers scent the air. He breathes in a dream of lovers.

Bewitched by his longing for the newer tempo, Shi-zheng blows cigarette smoke to expunge the perfumed breeze. A cloudy billowing stings, he winks one eye several times. He stops to suck in the last draught of nicotine, and he crushes the cigarette butt under the sole of his shoe.

Shi-zheng's heel scrapes grit. If he listened for more, he may also hear a ghostly saxophone blurt a note, but he is not contemplative. His choice is for the demolisher's percussion, the jack hammer and the ball. In 1961, when he is less than twenty and a student in America, Shi-zheng senses a malaise that makes him irritable with Penang.

Detached and moody, he strides to the small staircase leading from the corridor across the sprung dance floor through glass doors to the foyer. Not wishing to spend time soaking up the ambience those Armenians, the Sharkie brothers, had recessed into the corners of the E & O, he barks at the dilatory receptionist who leaps out of his day-long sleep, startled eyes widening, blinking blood-shot inquiry before surlily acceding to Shi-zheng's demands.

Glancing to his right to check the state of play, the would-be developer sees to his left a vision of the streets he will mobilise, towers shadowing the sea and the town. He flings himself into his Vanguard. He throws the gear stick to blast the languor heavily settled over Northam Road. He heads off to a shop on China Street where he will secure a deal for crawler tractors at the same time as he will arrange for the demise of some minor competition. A racehorse owner of little consequence was impeding but not preventing his uncle's investment in West Australian real estate.

Wang Shi-zheng is singular. He is pre-eminent on the leather upholstery of his car sliding at midday under white heat. He would love to walk on the wild side of life, but he worked out long ago that Chinese boys could never lounge and pout like James Dean or Marlon Brando. His bony body, he acknowledges, looks best when fully clothed, his face impassively jade still. His has the delicate lineaments of a transsexual, lending him a decadent beauty that will lose its refinements with age. That he breathes for power whistles strength through his bones, extinguishing doubts that may arise from droll self-deprecation.

It is likely he is avoiding the denouement of his story by roaring through the side of it, choosing to rip with the desert wind tunnelling between the tower blocks of the equatorial town his developments will create. Are these the scorched disfigurements signalling his future?

Only the alert will see him striding behind the walls of his own making. Not his father, but those fish, wide-eyed by rocks, idling between weeds. The crows circling over the garbage dumped at the back of a *yum-cha* restaurant on the day his uncles praised him for doing so well at his studies will screech for him.

Neither the mound of garbage nor the *yum-cha* restaurant were there when Li-tsieng, relaxed after making love to Rose all afternoon, took his roll of film to the hotel's photography shop. Because he wanted the film developed before twenty-four hours passed, he paid a bankroll of notes across the counter. His Uncle BK would have burst with apoplexy if he had seen the profligate way this boy, the family embarrassment, casually handed the money to the sleek Japanese photographer who sold a complete range of camera equipment at the shop. He was the photographer mostly seen with his cameras at weddings and the races and fancy dress parties and all the other social functions held at the sporting clubs. He was the one who painstakingly assembled collections of portraits of those people of Penang the Kempetai would want to recognise — like the one of Rose, an attractive young woman a military gentleman might find useful.

Li-tsieng passed the florist's and the beautician's, taking in a draught of air poisoned with delapilatory lotion, and the barber's whose soap and shaving cream scented the place where a few rickshaws rested their front wheels or shafts against the footpath. He sank into the hooded and screened cabin of one. There, in the shadowed interior, the complacency that had styled him a fop and a wastrel, a good-for-nothing living off the family's well-earned wealth, dipped down to bend under the weight of something new stirring in his heart.

When he saw Uncle Cho's Rover ploughing up Penang Road, Li-tsieng instructed the rickshaw man to peddle a circumlocutory route down a side lane leading off Argyll Street and a series of back streets off Burmah Road through another network of lanes and side paths to Gurney Drive and home. He gathered in his body a strength of feeling he never thought possible for him to have for another human being. It was such a new sensation, its impact weakened him. When he stood to pay the rickshaw driver, he swayed unsteadily. The man thought he was drunk. He peddled away without giving Li-tsieng the change for the dollar bill he crumpled in his fist. It was then Li-tsieng understood what he had to do.

That he took a sea voyage to Chile and back again to make good his resolution demonstrates the great shift that took place under and through his heart after he took the photographs of Rose. Knowing, as he did, his family expected him to abandon her to fate or whatever may be worse than death,

Li-tsieng was suddenly inspired to know he had, in the downturned palms of his folded and gloved hands, one part in life to play. And that was with Rose.

Shi-zheng?

He is not the sort to take it easy. He is running the palm of one hand over his smooth hair, another two or three years of college life in America glimmering dimly, and he is thinking how to manoeuvre the dispute between the City Council of Penang and the State Government of the Province of Wellesley over the Low Cost Housing Committee his family's way.

Anyway, who is he, this Shi-zheng?

Is he a poet, extolling freedom's virtues over a cappuccino in a city cafe? Is he a pair of shoes scuffing rubble and retreating down a street he threatens to make again? Or is he a universal phenomenon, a new age airport man born with a precious spoon in his mouth and a calculator for a brain?

Flying from Santiago to Penang, Harvard-Bonn-Paris-Rome-Tokyo-Beijing, does he speak Spanish, Malay, Hokkien, English, German, French, Japanese and some Italian, Cantonese and Mandarin? If, by breaking idioms over twisted meanings, language pronounces any kind of identification at all within the world, what does being multi-lingual do to his identity? How can he be defined?

Does anonymity subvert him? Fracture him? Camouflage him?

Maybe it does, for his is the face passing through the universities, running between the lecture hall and the library, mouth returning quick smiles with greetings in the words he learned just yesterday of a language studied for years among the noises of another country. He bows over his desk, his books and the footpaths winding round the grounds of his learning, and he hopes he is not too conspicuous, choosing carefully from the fashions, styles and colours readily absorbed into the background without altering anyone's imaging of the environment.

Regardless of his aptitude, his lecturers will condemn him for his egoism. They will lean over the faculty bar with their beers and red wines, explaining him to each other. They will deplore his inability to socialise and criticise his lack of participation in tutorials, because they have no idea how nuances escape him. Nor will they think to ask him how difficult it is to speak loudly and with utter conviction after years of observing rules nourishing a lack of candour. Perhaps they disparage him, agreeing he is a gutter rat, out for his own survival. They do not understand his is the new reality, that is to say, he knows he should survive at all costs.

This Shi-zheng may have been ahead of his time, a precursor to a newer, simpler set of paradigms. As early as the 1960's, this Shi-zheng knows to reinvent himself again and again. Daily. To fit in with the others whose faces break up like his own. And he unmakes his creation to accommodate the strangers whose pale eyes sink backwards into depths he cannot fathom, seeing horizons inside his light bones and searching for frontiers under his skin. Troubled by their scrutiny, he will avert his eyes and receive the sensation of their hostilities he names too easily, and he will fold a protective coolness round the possibility of anger for fear it will get the better of him.

And forever and forever and forever he will make another one of himself — for the benefit of relatives speaking languages he does not readily follow; for the accountants in boardrooms where numeracy takes precedence over words; and, wrapping himself in newspapers, for his eyes feasting on political indicators pointing up the instability of moneyed trends.

Shi-zheng.
Unmade.
Remade.
Made over and over again.

From the beginning, he curled round his chest.

Squabbling women filled a steaming kitchen. There were the little girls, maids, some would say slaves, who were caned often, and there were women with special numerical designations he had to remember — grandmothers, mothers, aunts and sisters. His mother, a tolerated invalid, was his father's only wife. She was his First Mama. But his grandmother was his grandfather's third wife — she was Shi-zheng's Third Grandma. Instead of letting his eyes wander apprehensively from adult face to adult face, fearfully anticipating their rivalry for power, Shi-zheng drew right down inside himself where he could grip the meaning of a dialogue between equations.

The video continuously obliterates daily indiscretions threatening harmony by replaying others fighting more dramatic battles. This continuous interruption of domestic moments leaches our memories. We forget our past accounted for many loves that were not sexual, those interdependencies far more complicated than a tee vee drama can capture. The images forming part of those fictions reeling into living rooms remind us, for most of this world's people, family disgusts and holds firm.

Shi-zheng, if prompted, would say his first memories were mathematical calculations worked out under a conveniently placed inlaid ebony dresser, one his Straits Chinese family took with them from Penang to Santiago. Other memories were of Third Grandma. He may not let on how she spoiled him with sweets and fine clothes, or how grateful he was for the way she protected him when he was small.

When the family ire was up, and the aunts took it on themselves to be spiteful about his malingering mother, they made it seem his birth had caused her invalidity. If he committed a misdemeanour — if he stayed out too long with the Chilean boys after school, waited in the church cloister to see what the Catholic priests did with the incense burner, or lingered at the markets where people speaking in a long loud riverrun struck bold attitudes like characters in movies — then all those women, the grandmothers and mothers and aunts, liked to hint how like his rotten father he was. They said that, like his despicable father, he strayed too far. Third Grandma would intervene, sometimes quietly taking him out of their way, other times scolding them for uttering harmful remarks about the dead.

No one during these tribal wars ever spoke his father's name.

Third Grandma smelt of roses.

She was not old.

When he watched her sitting over her embroidery or standing beside her bedroom window to look through lace curtains down on the street where the people of Santiago promenaded, he saw how her beauty was unawakened, locked in its youth, too still and melancholy. She was not like the vibrant women at the markets. They kicked up bright flounced skirts. Above their flashing eyes, they swung vivid shawls and tossed manes of hair. Their bodies leapt with life and stank of sweat and sex.

Third Grandma smelt of roses.

Her face, her body, was as beautiful and as still as jade, a quality he shared with her, but with masculine advantage. He understood his body, the gender of it, saved him from being locked up in metaphor. It saved him from mooning at windows where he saw she languished. Perhaps his family would define him, but it would never immure him as it did her.

And yet, she was not without clout. From within the intricate latticework of Wang intra-familial relationships, Third Grandma made known her tiny determination that he should receive some benefit from the family coffers. She petitioned senior uncles to request on her behalf that her husband should see to the education of the boy.

Her formality was inspired.

Her husband said he loved her graciousness.

The boy, seemingly a good boy, bowed his head, but not from gratitude for grandmotherly graciousness nor for grandfatherly generosity. Shi-zheng promised himself not to subside under the will of others. Money maketh the man, someone said in his hearing, and Shi-zheng loved the maths that made it. His head filled with equations in currencies he saw looped round the world, he bowed for the pleasure of his vision.

His school results found their way into his grandfather's study. Twice the old man asked to see him.

Junior uncles rushed around the Patriarch's offices. They dressed in cream suits. They attempted to sport a Chilean bravado, but their mustachios refused to grow ostentatiously bushy. These young dandies contented themselves with red carnation buttonholes, flashy handkerchiefs drooping from their back pockets and hair slicked straight back over their ears and off their foreheads. They took care to make their mouths petulant.

Standing with his back to the door, the boy kept his head down and his hands behind his back.

Coughing slightly in the manner of an English gentleman, the Patriarch, a Chinese of the Federated Malay States, a Straits Chinese, a *baba*, shuffled some papers and began to speak quietly about understanding the secret code of being upright. He exhorted his grandson to believe that he, as Patriarch, was a creature born to integrity blessed with the ability to recognise the greater profundities in life, the better burden of which was to bring justice to an unstable and sometimes capricious world. This he interspersed with a comment or two about "These good marks! Excellent, I should say!" Within the homily on distinguishing, in foreign parts, between discretion and valour, he suggested the boy should go to university. "In the United States. The new arbiter," he said. "It's a modern world, now." He believed the boy's English was more than adequate.

The boy saw clean trouser cuffs above shining laced leather shoes. The socks were triangularly patterned in English brown wool. Instantly he constructed equations linking the co-relative factors of the triangles. For no one needed to explain to Shi-zheng patterns overlapping patterns, spinning kaleidoscopically and understood mathematically described the new reality — his grandfather's 'modern world'. Let it be said the grandfatherly socks revealed patterns in the 1950's reinvented as the modules ascribed to the stock exchanges' smart turning around of vast sums of money. Shi-zheng did not live to see his futures come undone in October 1986.

Back then, in the past tense, an old voice roamed around the room. When the old man's hand cupped his shoulder, Shi-zheng saw the trousers and the shoes had moved. The hand was not heavy and gripping, it was kind. Shi-zheng stood ramrod still. He waited to be dismissed. His grandfather smiled distantly, and nodded. The boy backed out of the room, his fingers at his back thumbing digits figuring the triangles he wanted to put into an action. His was an engrossed, bowed head.

Rolled over like that, he bowled clean around the world.

Shi-zheng, rushing round North America, heard the deep twanging of the electric guitar, reminding him he had a heart that beat. He found women who wore tight straight skirts. Above their tight pastel sweaters, he thought he saw how their cool eyes calculated profit and loss. Fascinated, he watched the way they swung free soft hair. And when they were alone with him, he discovered their sinuous bodies smelt headily of nutmeg and fish.

In his student flat, he leaned against a graffiti-patterned fridge with a radio balanced on its top among bottled sauces, opened noodle packets and half-eaten loaves of sliced white bread, the deep throat of the south ripping into the centre of his head singing about women and love. But neither Jerry Lee Lewis nor doe-eyed student companions diverted Shi-zheng from those figures braiding landmass to landmass clear around the globe. He bolted past rhythm 'n' blues and sexually alert women for the neat columns of actuarial studies.

He sat at a university library desk overlooking the panorama the United States of America spreads out to indulge visionaries. He played a hard game of tennis, and he shot a bull's eye at the pistol club, and he drove the golf ball exactly into its flagged hole. Nothing should be wasted, time after all is said and done, is money, and these sports prepared him to make money at his leisure.

His American colleagues forgot to see how he was different — black hair, stiff and straight. Lips, too full, a mouth too wide, nose squashed against a flattened face, ginger brown eyes small and slanted. They saw and mostly accepted him as a hybrid — someone who was not quite like them and yet one among them.

For him, their perception of him was not completely irrelevant. He was alert to their moods. He accommodated himself to their humour. He linked their emotions to himself through their music. But long ago Shi-zheng had made pacts with himself. He would play their game according to his rules. He would play to win. Ruthlessly.

His senior uncles, BK and Cho, asked him to take some university breaks in Penang where they could reassure themselves he was worthy of the family's generosity and good will. Barely conscious their world was slowly changing its course, they entered the Penang Swimming Club by the door the Hainanese staff in earlier days guarded for Europeans only, and they sat at tables over whisky and mahjong. They discussed share dealing, the latest prostitute to delight the town's *towkays*, and their long held vision for a bridge linking the island with the mainland. Self-righteously folding gold ringed fingers over stomachs fattened on the best *nyonya* dishes the Straits could offer, these men agreed the boy was an asset no family other than their own was blessed with.

Fish, hearing this, swam in circles, agitating a ghost that rolled heavily in the silt.

Down Lorong Chulia, Shi-zheng found an enthusiast for the technology that would reduce the world to a microdot, making bridges needless. He had read an Argentinian short story by Jorges Luis Borges about the future explorers. They would be scholars who would travel into outer space to the oldest satellites where libraries stored depositories of information on pinheads that sages would study. The knowledge found would be new for being so old and complicated and enigmatic. He liked the technology in this story, which he dismissed as one that might fascinate romantics. At bottom, Shi-zheng would say he was a pragmatist.

Happily making it look as if he knew how to drink well and how to enjoy the services of a variety of local prostitutes, 'going with the boys' being his camouflage against the charge of Western individualism, his dreams were spangled with microdots linking satellites and beaming information from here to there, business he imagined dominating government. Unlike the proletariat shouting slogans demanding power down the 1960s along the streets and at the jail walls from Santiago to Singapore to Soweto, he saw his business would stealthily and rapidly take control of the universe.

Shi-zheng believed in *Goldfinger* more than he trusted Borges.

Fish gasped.

Something in history died.

Stepping in and out of her fictions, his aunt, Chin-pei, heard the mathematics of his soul. Criss-crossing the Straits between Belawan and Swettenham Port, leaving the distilled calm of the shores of Lake Toba for the journey to Medan down the coast to Kuala Lumpur then to Singapore for Santiago to see her elderly father, she saw the young man reading the newspapers and working a calculator. Later she saw him studying hook-ups.

His pace was not professorial.

Chin-pei saw flash before her eyes the story of her nephew glinting from scruffy head to sandalled feet, sweating in a loose shirt and wincing inside small workshops where he would hide his face with others like him behind cigarette smoke. But she did not write it down. Shi-zheng, she sensed, pillowed his head on figures moving around the universe, unambiguously transposing and recreating patterns, monochromatic mandalas in spiralled formation spinning through serial dramas to a big resolution, a deposit holding in the moneyed heaven of his own making.

For him, history concatenated, time drooled down a banker's wall, currency moved.

She liked the mathematics of the plot she believed directed Shi-zheng's story. But if the sum total of his soul were numbers, where would she find his character? His nature? The essence suggesting his inner life?

She discovered death worried him.

When Third Grandma lay in her bed suffering the pains of a terminal illness, he cowered in silence, afraid a vehemence might break through his mathematical defence. Her dressing table was cluttered with bottles of English Rose moisturisers and body lotions. At its centre, on a square of silk patterned with peonies and phoenixes was her large box of rose scented powder. Her pink powder puff sat neatly on its top. But another smell robbed the room of her perfumes, the cold sweet smell of death.

Shi-zheng scratched his larynx and prompted his voice to ask Third Grandma what his father had done wrong. Startled, Chin-pei stepped backwards. She heard her mother suck in her breath, and she heard herself thinking this one is full of pain. Rather than hear the moral tale of her brother's extravagance in love that cost him his life, she excused herself and quickly left the room.

Chin-pei missed seeing how still her mother lay, to gather her muscles to her frail bones.

Shi-zheng's not so old Third Grandmother slid out of her high lonely bed. She lowered her feet into embroidered and beaded pink silk slippers, and pushed her arms into a red gown with garlands of white and pink flowers embroidered down its silken back. Her fingers fumbled with the loops buttoning the gown from her throat to below her knees. Tiredly but correctly dressed for her grandson's company, she settled on a small velvet covered stool in front of a bedside table so ornately painted with roses it looked like a garden itself.

He knew she liked roses. But he did not know why roses were special for her.

In a slow motion that made Shi-zheng giddy to watch, she slid open the top drawer of her bedside table to lift out a book covered with watermark silk. She pressed it to her lips before she opened it reverentially. Passing her hand across one photograph, she bid Shi-zheng to look at an elegant young man dressed in a pin-striped suit, a yellow rosebud pinned to his buttonhole. A top hat and a walking cane overlapped his gloved hands. "This is your father, " she whispered. Shi-zheng looked at this man Third Grandma pointed at, the one she said was his father. He was surprised to see he shared a look with those people from the Santiago markets, something sensual he had not expected. Third Grandma said, "He is punished."

Shi-zheng looked closely at her soft face. The tears beaded in the corners of her fading eyes. He face twisted. He looked down at his hands, and he folded them over hers, resolving not to ask for any more story telling.

A skeletal finger stroked his heart, thumbing its pliancy.

Catching sight of his smarting eyes when he left the room, Chin-pei felt his heart vibrate behind his pallid face.

He was, during those last days of her mother's life, Chin-pei's nearest companion. He rarely spoke. His eyes grappled with grief above columns of newspaper print, spiking details of politics and the Bourse. He spotted indicators thrusting through durable and transitory indices. Chin-pei guessed he was the type who wanted others to think he did not have it in him to share a moment of grief with his aunt. She understood for him numeracy was love's substitute.

There was one night, late in the 1960s, when she was in Penang to welcome him back from where he had been, Chin-pei heard a call. It may have been a saxophone horning a sad bar skyward. Shi-zheng looked up to hear the eerie note wafting across the seawall of the family's post-war house. She listened, and she let the haunting sound ride over her loneliness. From habit, she felt the unravelling of story she no longer wrote down.

She leaned back in her wicker chair to gaze at the moon. Ferns frothed around her. Crickets and other insects sang. The sea at low tide gently lapped the shore. This scene was cinematic, this ambience searched out by Warner Bros panning for mood to elaborate an intricate story she knew, perhaps by Somerset Maugham. Bette Davis played the spurned lover in one, *The Letter*, in which the moon and the clouds had their role.

But a chair scraping over the tiled floor of the terrace startled her. She sat straight up. Shi-zheng stuffed his hands in his pockets and stalked, head bowed, straight out of the garden. His footsteps resounded throughout the house. After a minute or two, a door banged. A car engine varoomed.

The ferns nodded.

The sea lapped and lapped and, after ruffling an unsteady silence, crashed.

Chin-pei, leaning back to look once more at the full moon, preferring to look directly at its silvery light than at the moon-lit garden, reflected on her young nephew. She sensed the pulse of his reality concealed inside skin made to mimic seamlessness. A poet? A pair of shoes? A new age airport man? She imagined him bent over circuit boards and lists of tickertape.

Shi-zheng was less enigmatic than he was an enigma. His image of himself unmade and about to be remade and made over and over again, he was devoid of colour and all the more anonymous because of that.

Like money.

♓

9. *a nib for a shoe*

For the girl Chin-pei, writing stories was an affirmation of good will in the liquid transience of life.

In the late afternoon when the sea mirrored the sky, Chin-pei listened to the sounds of life's distractions. French grammars and dictionaries shelved by her study's desk merged into a shadow as one. The novel she was reading, its pages open beside her notebook, took on a lunar mauve.

Seagulls squabbled. A servant harangued and harangued and harangued a child, a husband, a fellow servant, the harsh syllabary of Hokkien driving a metallic wedge into the depths of Chin-pei's father's garden. Sea lapped and thudded the wall, vainly to be heard. A fishing trawler may have honked its nightly farewell. And somewhere deep in the house, a record slipped from its covers, dropped onto a turntable, the first bars of an invitation to dance growling under the needle, hesitant to jolly in the allegro, waiting as if for a finger to snap on a yellow electric light.

But Chin-pei was not drawn by the changes in diurnal light. She turned her foot to examine the red leather of a new shoe. Her father had explained these were her last until peace was declared which, in those mid-months of 1941, she had no reason to doubt would be soon. Stylish French footwear was her greatest love. She appraised the stitching of its strap passing through a tiny buckle high on her instep, and she listened for the sound of Li-tsieng on the staircase. Her brother should return, she expected, from his mistress, this latest one troubling more than his wife who sulked in her bedroom all day. For it was whispered in the kitchen and hissed in the corridors and astutely avoided by the men who discussed world affairs in the submarine dining hall of the family mansion, this one was English, the niece of a respected man about town.

Chin-pei wanted to go to Paris. The Nazi occupation, she believed, would not destroy its energy, its spirit.

To pass the time of its humiliation, she began to write detective stories in French based on her knowledge of the city gleaned from novels and fashion magazines. She poured over street maps. She pictured steam condensing on the windows of seedy bars. She imagined a clientele whose downward curling hat brims met flicked up collars and hunched up shoulders. A lone woman hitched furs round her hips and pouted under street lamps. A wisp of smoke coiled from her reddened mouth.

A saxophone bleated, and Chin-pei's moon lit a cobbled street.

Shadowy figures scurried down flights of steps into cellars and through double doors opening onto a close or a mews, down a street or a little rear lane, up poorly lit staircases to rooms filled with mirrors and inestimable paintings and women whose stylishness attracted the attention of smooth-headed men. Champagne glasses clinked. The froufrou of silk rustled under the intermittent rumbling of one man's deep baritone. The treble of women's light laughter, spiking a clipped assertion of fact, contrasted with the cautious murmuring of received and approved opinion, and all the voices joined in the hushed and beautifully phrased orchestral piece of well-modulated intelligent conversation.

A woman, more beautiful than the other incomparable women slinking through Chin-pei's stories, flicked long red fingernails, a signal for the room to empty of its glamour. Rapidly it did, and across a wall full of paintings slipped one shadowy man wearing two-toned shoes and a sheen to his slicked black hair.

The light shut down.

A fat man who thought his fingers were running over a woman's bare shoulder froze. It was then Fat Man realised his mistake — that she had evaporated, as had all the evening's company. Fat Man's face fell. It twisted anguish with vulnerability and awful aloneness, and the terrible self-judgement that he found himself to be foolish. In the fracturing of a second, a crook flashed a knife and thrust it between those fat covered ribs. Blood gurgled across expensive carpet.

A door swung open. A triangle of blue light and a saxophone's final note spilled over silvered cobbles. Into the soaring silence of the music's resolution, the door slammed shut. A man wearing two-toned shoes and a sheen to his slicked black hair walked quickly into the shadowless dark.

A foggy wisp vaporised beneath a fire escape's steel struts. A woman with a lion's mane of hair swung her foot as if she traced a goetic circle into the greased dust of a city's streets. Perhaps the man's erotic imagination, directing his negotiations with the woman, distracted him so that he did not see a blue pin-striped back vanish between buildings. Certainly, she reported with some surprise a flashing brightness as if a UFO had landed where the back of a pair of patent leather heels, the type that go with two-toned shoes, fast retreated down an unlit tunnel.

For the pair, the order of their world — the moon lighting a cobbled street, the black space of buildings hulking up against a starless sky, the exchange of money for skin on skin slitheriness — had been threatened and took a slight shaking before it settled again.

They may have heard a tiny heel scrape over gravel followed by the sound of a man's retreating footsteps. Of this, they were not certain. When questioned by detectives investigating a triad's execution, they agreed they heard nothing other than the high note of stiletto heels chipping damp stones. One pair. And if anyone else had been awake enough to lean from a window or look down from a balcony, they may have seen a tiny woman walk carefully across the watery black of dew wet cobbles. If that person was a keen observer, the blueblackness of her short hair may have caused a remark.

A rich man's death satisfied Chin-pei's plots. It validated her heroines chosen from a collection of Mata Haris spying for economic gain. With mathematical accuracy, Chin-pei plotted the demise of German rice kings, French thieves of Siamese religious treasures, British drug traffickers and Dutch rubber barons.

Police and detectives were given space to deceive each other. Their garlicky breaths steamed over the corpse. Together they assessed the triads' methods and shared their fears of 'inscrutable Orientals'. They stood with hands cupped out on the high round of their buttocks. Dispassionately, they surveyed the blood sprayed high up the walls, and observed how miraculously no paintings were damaged. They slunk into anterior rooms. They deduced the arty gathering all knew each other — no signs of struggle, no damaged window latches, no weapons wrapped in a bloodied handkerchief deposited among packing cases tossed out with the kitchen garbage.

A raffish detective distinguished by his rumpled suit and ill-kempt hair hung back from the policing gaggle. Something glittered beside his shoe's pointed toe. He bent, and he slipped into his pocket a diamond hair clasp in the shape of a sea-horse.

Chin-pei owned one of these.

She liked to slip it into her stories.

Stretching her leg and turning her ankle to admire the sheen of good leather on that evening of September in 1941 when she was just about seventeen, Chin-pei imagined her underworld shadow acting in Paris, the city she visited only in her dreams. That she may one day become equal to and perhaps surpass her own fictions was a thought too remote for one whose loyalty was filial, therefore simple.

Li-tsieng's affection for a yellow haired woman created in Chin-pei a difficult fidgetiness.

Li-tsieng began asking abrupt if indirect questions about the women she met at the afternoon teas organised by one of the European consul's wives in their family rooms. Sitting politely, enduring the boredom of these social events, Chin-pei adduced their value to the men of her clan, personalising contacts to enhance prestige. The men avoided the tedium of the hours. But if they were to maximise business by submitting her to this boredom, Chin-pei expected to benefit too.

Folding her hands and watching dust play across light, she learnt to memorise gestures, mannerisms, those hints establishing the distinctiveness of character. She was fascinated by the way one woman let her hand fall and spread across the sofa, then lean heavily into her words. Another woman gripped a lace handkerchief and stared at the ground by her feet where she dropped an unswervable opinion around which she tightened her whole body.

These laborious, cumbersomely large women were unalterably domestic. They neither knew nor appeared to care about world affairs. They expressed no interest in the arts, the sciences or business. If she asked a question about the artist of a painting of a bowl of flowers, or a horse's head or a group of large-eyed faces staring off the canvas at whoever could bear to stare back long enough, the women shrugged their shoulders. In their estimation, the artist was of no consequence. If she asked about the European war and its effect on the rubber industry or the availability of oil, commodities she shrewdly guessed would be in greater demand, they wearily deferred to their husbands' opinions.

They seemed to sleep where they sat on yellow chintz sofas, sliding fingers into silver engraved boxes from which they tiredly extracted cigarettes, perhaps bumping a tall alabaster table lamp or brushing a bare arm against a Siamese urn or a *nyonya* vase. Chin-pei despised them. They lacked control. To her, they were without merit, sex slaves and nannies in strange marriages contracted to legalise physical love. Like thieves, they robbed status from the performance of matrimony rather than bringing to the liaison any unseen advantages.

Their languid softness, their pink sweatiness, their drooping gentleness, and their inability to be intelligently informed, condemned them in her eyes.

Entirely out of malice, she wrote these women into her novels. They were decorative diversions and whores under lamp posts, both of nuisance value when she structured her plot around a diplomatic incident or, and this was her favourite plot, the gallery opening of a new artist's exhibition. Chin-pei was too young to understand that the women suffered a pervasive foreboding that they may one day be without country, and then they would no longer know who they were.

If she was too young to understand their placidity was fear, she learnt to listen carefully. For when these interminable occasions came to their sighing end, Chin-pei scribbled among descriptions of clothes and shoes and hairstyles and the colours of lipsticks and the quantity of red and white powder dusted on sweating faces, those turns of phrases and lists of words not readily found in dictionaries.

The wide ranging meanings of the word 'thing' was one of these.

In unguarded moments, the women gossipped about 'things'. It took Chin-pei some time to work out a 'thing' was the practice of making love with someone you were not married to, or a suspicion that this was happening.

Li-tsieng's questioning alerted her to Rose, the yellow haired one. She suspected he might want to have a 'thing' with if he was not already.

Rose was a pretty creature, she allowed, little different from the older women, Chin-pei thought, although she witnessed a sadness pin-pointed at the centre of her extraordinary blue eyes. Chin-pei guessed these eyes were the colour of cornflowers. She guessed right, charming the European women with an adroitly phrased yet transparently obvious question to confirm her lexicon was correct.

She reported to herself that Rose's smile was quite attractive.

Rose's chaperone, Aunt Margaret, dismayed Chin-pei. She was an exceedingly dim woman, over-fond of gin and tonic. To give her her due, these tea and coffee gatherings induced in Aunt Margaret a series of yawns followed by protestations like, "I must say ...! Oh Dear ...! Forgotten ...! Oh Dear Dear Dear!" Aunt Margaret, Chin-pei decided, was not such a bad, how would they say it? — old stick. Yes! Old stick. Probably an amusing 'old stick' in her own befuddled way.

Stifling yawns, eyes steady above the lip of her tea-cup, she watched the young woman sitting next to Aunt Margaret. Rose. She tried to picture this vapid yellow and blue girl in bed with her brother.

Chin-pei longed to confirm her images of imagined rooms. She wished she could see a European woman's bedroom. What would decorate the walls? Fall under the bed? Drop forgotten in corners? Would adjoining bathrooms filled with decanted bath oils and perfumes close behind embossed doors? Did powder float, white dust trailing from bathroom to bedroom? Were cushions, scattered over the bed, embroidered or edged with lace?

She could never ask Li-tsieng how Rose undressed. Where did she put her hat, her gloves and her handbag? Did she carry a bunch of flowers as European women sometimes did? What would she do with those? Hand them to a maid? Dump them in a vase? Or forget them on a table?

Did she slip off her shoes or kick them off? Did her feet smell? Were they sweaty? Did she roll her stockings down her legs or did she leave them on, only taking off her knickers? Did she break into song? Dance? Stare at him rudely in the direct way of Europeans? Grin? Like a monkey? And her other underthings. She wanted to get it right about removing clothes.

Chin-pei, substituting the nib of her pen for a beautiful pair of stiletto heeled shoes, set out to track down the bedroom habits in an imagined city where collars flicked up, the brims of hats curled down and shoulders, too slight to be French, hunched.

If events had taken a different turning, if there had been no war interrupting her family's life in Penang, if there had been no need to seek refuge in Chile, perhaps her history would have taken another course leading away from Khor Lu-hsien. Perhaps she would have married another ... perhaps, perhaps, perhaps! In the long history of women, matrimony is a one-way route. Chin-pei did not dispute it as such — she was not rebellious enough to imagine her life should divert off the matrimonial pathway walked down by centuries of women. Simply Chin-pei hoped for a future with a husband who would not ignore her the way her brother did his wife. Duty, and a respect for fate that had made her a woman, were tacitly accepted by her, not questioned. She was practical. Rebellion would only lead her to a quintessential aloneness entered by her into her French lexicon as *seul à seul*.

Anonymity, and nothingness.

This was a concept beyond the comprehension of one who understood she was like a peony growing in a splendid garden identified as the Wang family. She was first Wang, second Chin-pei. Not for her any grand acts like the crazed passion of Madame Bovary that spilled throughout a novel, a gross excess she rejected. Chin-pei conformed. She participated in the tranquillity of family life.

Not surprising, then, that without any opposition from within herself or from the families concerned, Khor Lu-hsien, a crook from Brazil with an ability to seduce her with shoes, married Chin-pei, in the goodness of time, that is.

And so, on the parapet of an Italianate mansion somewhere

in Santiago, a square of grease on Lu's thickly black hair gleaming by moonlight, he smiled for the pleasure of proposing marriage, the perfume of magnolias overwhelming the moment. He slipped onto her small feet fine red shoes, a diamond sea-horse snaking down the back of the high, narrow heels. He led her, teetering on the wickedly beautiful shoes, indoors where he presented her to the members of their families as his chosen wife. They beamed their goodwill, and they clapped their hands to announce to the world that this match was well-blessed. The wealth from both families was sound. These two, everyone agreed, would enjoy a propitious future, advancing the respectable sources of gain of both clans.

Chin-pei adored Lu-hsien. His teeth sparkled. His hair glinted. Whether casually dressed in linen and silk, commercially in black striped suits, a red carnation pinned to his lapel, or elegantly in tails, Lu-hsien glittered. He wore diamonds as his preferred accessory. He wore them as rings, tie-pins, shirt studs and cuff-links. Khor Lu-hsien lavished them on Wang Chin-pei.

Impressions gathered from old whodunits suggest a young woman leaning on an expensive man's arm is a sure sign of the *demi-mode*. In Penang, she did not like to go to the picture houses, but Lu-hsien loved the big time glamour of movies about crooks. He took her to them in downtown Santiago. From them, the scene Chin-pei learnt to create was the one where the fine-limbed Chinese girls slinked in *cheong-sams* and pouted over whisky and bourbon on ice.

If Chin-pei's whodunits ever made it to the cinema, an emblem of crookery confirmed in words would have coincided with the visual cliché, repeated for millions of hours, of a steamy Chinatown full of staircases, other people's laundry and pouting women silkily wriggling their hips, elaborate cigarette holders fixed with Russian Soubranies extending their small painted fingernails.

When her plot shifted to more expensive places — the club bars and the discreet restaurants — she had men with oiled hair brush lips over feminine hands. The men spied their rivals, reflected in mirrors arranged behind potted palms, sliding out to catch a last gasp of fresh air. It was a scene she liked to create and recreate with a few variations. If the crook got the crook, well and good, and if the garlic-reeking constabulary caught either one, the equation closed with its answer. It was the mathematics of plot, elaborately embroidered, some would say padded, with contemporary political detail that she loved to elaborate.

Alone in her Santiago boudoir, Chin-pei the writer lingered to describe a man's oiled hair inclining over a slender woman's apparently submissive gaze. The woman was herself, Chinese and beautifully small. Chin-pei exaggerated the effect. The gangster's moll cast her eyes at her man's feet. The smile, its creator understood, was more knowing than shy. She pointed the toe of her shoe daintily, and the diamond-studded heel winked a wicked light. This gangster's moll, reflecting Chin-pei's ironic vision of herself, well displayed her man's ability to acquire wealth.

True to say, from one angle, her caricature of herself was not strikingly different from her description of those women she so despised who were of a race other than her own. All the same, it would be inaccurate to dismiss her as a decorative diversion on whose body Lu conspicuously displayed his wealth. Chin-pei was more than an adornment to be adorned. She was Lu's partner. She stepped in and out of her fictions, criss-crossing from what seemed to be an acceptance of the everyday to writing in an atmosphere of distilled calm a range of observations that made her detective stories complicit with the real.

But history stole the march on her well-shod feet.

After peace was declared, the party above the magnolias in Santiago stopped. The diamonds were less in evidence, discreetly sparkling from a finger or a wrist, the more ostentatious brooches and stomachers and finely studded footwear packed away in bank vaults or cashed in for gold bullion.

Chin-pei sailed for Medan in North Sumatra with the understanding she and Lu would assist claiming back the Wang's pre-war interests. When the links from Penang to Medan to Port Dickson were re-established, Lu dealt in military hardware. He smuggled the big stuff — tanks, trucks, jeeps — across the Straits and back again, selling to the Sumatran gangs engaged in a fight for an independent Indonesia. And he sold to the obdurate Dutch who refused to relinquish the emerald islands of their former colony until 1949.

Balancing her loyalty between her father and her husband, and from behind a screen of managerial relatives, Chin-pei arranged for women labourers on coffee estates within the Wang sphere of interest to pack small arms and ammunition into the beans bundled on their heads. The women, barefooted and dressed in rough shirts and sarongs, walked with their loaded burdens down the tracks ribboning the estates to the crossroads at the base of the foothills. From sheds leaning under trees, their goods were transferred to trucks destined to journey through the nights to the highest bidder.

Chin-pei, her diamond studded evening shoes sealed in a bank vault in Santiago waiting for her to resume her extravagant life, discovered she liked playing diplomatic games with the bandits occupying Sumatran villages. One day they were respectable soldiers buying arms for their Nationalist struggle; the next, criminals she betrayed to the Dutch. She liked to turn the screw, so to speak. She lacked affection for the players, preserving any sentiment she may have had for the mathematical niceties of transforming her lived drama into the plot of a novel.

Story-lines plentifully supplied themselves. The pace was slow. There were no trysts by wrought iron lamp posts, no sudden disappearances down staircases or upwards into attics. In Medan, there were no bars or cellar doors to slam shut at midnight. The streets were dusty, not cobbled or macadamised to take the light percussion of tapping high heels. Headlights did not shaft down tunnelled streets. They blurred foggily down avenues of plantation trees and faded into the purpling swirl of primeval jungles. These tropical, indeed equatorial, stories unfolded as if exposure relieved the principals. The heat dissipated energy and peeled away the layers of intrigue usefully employed to disguise a fact or a face.

Yet, her cool regard was to come undone.

Flitting behind her eyes the evening she saw Hari Hutagalung's hand fly up to still her maid's shriek was an instantly visualised plot. Hari Hutagalung wore no down-turned brim or upturned collar. He walked proudly in a loose shirt and baggy trousers. His eye was clear, his bearing proud. He was a teacher and a writer, the kind of subversive poet political assassins have a habit of murdering. He had had enough of Dutch and Japanese prisons. He had had enough of politics. He wanted out.

He needed protection.

She grasped the hand proffered to shake hers.

She asked the maid to make him comfortable in a guest-room. Generously providing him with fresh clothing, she asked that he should be patient. She knew of an Australian who may be sympathetic enough to help a dissident poet escape the Dutch. He upturned his palms to show her he was in her hands, and he settled down to read her French novels and English newspapers.

In her later life, Chin-pei withdrew to Prapat, a town in the highlands of North Sumatra, her body emptied of its remorse and no longer aching. She rocked above the broad waters of Lake Toba with no clear recollection of the Australian's name. The fact that she did not know it rang with accusations of carelessness down the years, never failing to surprise her. Her memory had been trained to observe details for later scribbling, and her memory had failed her on this most vital day.

Was it Henson?

Or Hense?

She called him Hensby. He came with a companion. Both of them turned up on her doorstep. Little was said to establish that they were there on business.

Seated comfortably on cushioned rattan chairs, Hensby quietly allowed his companion to distract her.

Ricki, for that is who the companion said he was, smelt of the jungle. He laughed about killings. The maid, hearing how a body ripped up and the blood and guts sprayed and little globules of grey brain slimied his shirt front, dropped the tray of refreshments she carried in front of Chin-pei. Whipping her hands round to the front of her sarong, she bowed her head and sped back to the kitchen.

Hari Hutagalung, sitting in the guest-room, paused in his reading of *Le Mythe de Sisyphe*. He pressed his ear to the door, and listened attentively to cadences of brutish speech. His dark brown eyes circling hazel flecks outward to grey rims stared at a dull wall and transferred their insight of his passage to freedom to the sagging sensation of going nowhere. Mesmerised by his body's knowledge that he was soon to be extinguished, he forgot he stood behind a closed door, forgot his fingers curled round a book, forgot his middle finger lodged between pages 100 and 101. Hari forgot to conceal himself under a cover of total silence. The voice boasted about battles, first with the Japanese Imperial Army and then with the Royal Dutch forces and then with the Indonesian Nationalists. The man whose boasts he heard through the door was a mercenary, a soldier of fortune, one who followed wars for the love of strategy, hunting, killing. Hari's fingers released the book. It whacked on the tiled floor.

Hensby's eyelids flickered. He seemed to listen to his friend's story. Chin-pei watched how his smile fixed when his yellow eyes registered the papery whack that exposed a wanted man, one who loved freedom and stood to exist by himself, a man possibly waking from a trance, sweatily shivering with fear behind a door in a bedroom of a Chinese woman's house.

Somehow, his reserve hypnotised her. His murmuring lips spelt the discretion she believed she sought. She slipped him the name of the man who solicited her help, for whom she committed to memory the name of a ship to embark from Belawan, the seamy harbour town servicing Medan. Hensby's eyes slid under their fleshy lids. His pink lips rolled into a smile of sorts, and his fleshy jowls rose up and down his cheeks as he swallowed.

When Chin-pei woke gasping and sweating from pictures of brutal slayings flashing as if the action of a novel whipped through her sleep, dread prickled her skin. She learnt to fear a growing belief that Hensby and Ricki were not as they said they were. Hard slow days dogged hard slow days. Rumours reeled out from the kitchen. Finally, she was given the news that her client's bullet-ridden body was found dumped in a river.

Nausea hit the roof of her mouth and stunned her eyeballs. Fearful for her husband, fearful a revenge killing to punish her would end Lu's glimmering successes, Chin-pei fumbled chopsticks. She twisted congealed noodles in her bowl.

Lu was found dead in a rough lane near Belawan. He was stripped of his diamond ring. His skin was flayed. Hearing the news, anguish froze her spine. Her eyes hurt from tears too dismayed to flow.

She saw no more of Hensby, nor of his side-kick, the part Japanese, part Thai mercenary who introduced himself as Ricki. She heard mutterings from the kitchen that a British agent, perhaps an Australian national, had something to do with both these murders. But she asked no questions of anyone, sought no clarifying information. Speechless with grief, she retreated into a long mourning.

From within a circle of uncles and cousins and brothers, Chin-pei continued to smuggle. She dealt in cars stolen from Malaya, transported across the Straits to refurbishing plants in North Sumatra then back again for resale in Malaya. She plotted novels in which the collars turned up, hat brims dipped low, a woman's tiny heel clipped paving stones. But the stories dribbled, unfinished. Her passion for them had waned.

The last thing she remembered of that evening in 1941 before the family sailed for Chile was the gleam of her shoe when she pointed her toe to the floor and rolled her foot from side to side. The end of the day faded and darkened, then lightened with the happy ascent of the moon. She cradled her chin with one hand and held a pen in the other, watching, seemingly smiling at the sheen of her shoe as if entranced by the quality of good leather. The way the world was rotating, spinning, braiding her life through the events of a history revolving within a larger earth-shattering history was too momentous to consider.

She was little disturbed by her father's decision to take them all. He had the entire family of mothers and aunts and concubines and brothers and uncles and cousinly retainers packed up and bound for Chile. "Peace," he conjectured, "was a long way off."

"When peace comes back to us, the world won't be the same," he said.

Chin-pei had absolute faith in her father's wisdom. She

respected him too much to believe anyone should disobey him by the unethical pursuit of self-gratifying love. And thus it was that she could not believe Li-tsieng when he confided his longing to stay with the English woman. His audacity exposed a creature believing love for the yellow haired Rose existed more consequentially than a thread of smoke briefly curling before dissolving into the nothing of air.

The moment a record, spinning far away in the house, took up a smile, and the forlorn Li-tsieng left her alone, Chin-pei swung both her beautiful shoes under her desk. She wrote out in French the fast swelling of a new story recessed in an imagined Parisian underworld where men, glinting from oiled heads to two-toned shoes, traipsed. They hunched in big coats, collars flicked up, hat brims tipped down. They stuffed their hands in deep pockets. They winced under lamp posts, and shied into shadows. They hid their faces behind a smoky screen made of their own cigarillos.

A small woman, a diamond sea-horse pinned to her glossy black hair, clicketty-clicked onto a darkened street.

The men thundered up staircases. They cowered along walls. They swivelled through doorways. They grouped round large leather topped desks. They leant forward in chairs. They crossed ankles over knees. They picked their fingernails. Their fat boss played with a stationery sword. He congratulated them for a 'job well done' and cursed them for 'getting the case wrong'. Either way, their shocking murders were dumped in the Seine.

When Li-tsieng's recorded lyric stopped appraising a blue moon, a knife flashed, a man groaned, a pool of blood oozed across the moon's wash.

And a small shoe's sole scraped across a city's grit.

♓

10. *with no foothold anywhere,*

In Penang, round the traps so to speak, Rose had a 'reputation'.

On the basis of hearsay, some would say gossip, she was assigned to a boxed-in group over the caption 'wanton' which made it possible for the more pernicious to think she was 'a loose bit' an army officer could play with. There were more people than Rose could have known who had all the facts, that she was the mistress of a prominent but youthful Chinese, Wang Li-tsieng. They knew, too, that after Wang sailed away, Rose did not appear too downhearted. These people saw a girl carelessly dancing away the hours. They heard her flippant laughter. They swapped reported sightings of her cuddling up to the army boys. They did not see how painfully Rose existed in triplicate.

By special courier, Li-tsieng sent her a medium-sized print of the photograph he took of her in a slipper satin evening gown.

Rose was made both anxious and irritated that he should risk exposing her to her aunt and uncle by dispatching presents to the house in Dunn Street. To avoid answering any questions asked by Aunt Margaret, and with more exasperation than skill, she hurried the package into her bedroom where she briefly glanced at this picture of herself peeping coquettishly over her shoulder before sliding it inside its silk embroidered envelope then under her neatly folded and lightly perfumed knickers and things.

That was when she saw the note. At her feet. It had slipped out of the envelope and fallen on the floor. Bending to pick it up, her fingers, suddenly bloodless and hesitant, fumbled. Thumbing the folded paper, she sat down and the bed heaved to cushion her weight. Bouncing gently, her eyes skidded over the words.

A redness swelled inside her head. The words dipped away, her mouth dried up, but she forced her eyes to scratch across each syllable. In this way, she reread the note and she took in its meaning. Rose blinked. She lay back on the silk embroidered coverlet, her body swelling with emptiness, her skin clammy and chilled.

The housemaid found her, lying quite still, and staring, blank eyed, at the wall. The maid saw no tears on Rose's cheeks. Knowing a certain young man had sailed out of Penang with his family that morning, she hurried to find Cookie who waddled into the room, wiping his hands and, after one look at her strangely distorted expression, he called for the housekeeper. That bustling loquacious woman, Meena's mother, felt the girl's clammy forehead. Circling her wrist with thin, strong fingers, she ordered that a brew of herbs should be distilled in the kitchen.

"Cooling," she prescribed. "Too much heating! She can not take!"

The stuff was sour. Rose speedily fell into a troubled sleep. When she woke, she lay between coverlets, her body cold and weightless and numb. Her mouth, dried like thin paper, tasted old.

If someone told her she was sailing in miniature, her face mounted in a pale pigskin wallet flattened against Li-tsieng's chest, she would have smiled, thinking but not saying, "So that's where I am!" But in herself, she was a ghost. Her fractured spirit deprived her of sensations only half her head was able to register.

In her catatonic state, she felt dispossessed of her body. Her limbs, swinging in dance, she somehow observed objectively as if they were not hers. Stretching her mouth in laughter, she failed to recognise her face in the ugly grimace.

Her body, embraced by bulky boys under tropical moons blackening the shadows in moist gardens, was absent.

The gossips, and some uninterested observers, watched and saw in her happy sociability a girl out for a good time. They failed to understand — they could not see to appreciate — how ripped in two Rose felt. That was why those people who knew about Li-tsieng's liaison with Rose judged her heartless.

And then there was the largest photograph, the one the historian, Gillian Hindmarsh, found interleaved with building applications and old newspapers in the archives held at the Dewan Sri Penang. It remained the property of the photographer who developed the film for Li-tsieng. Confident in his knowledge of the future, Yokota Ryuichi filed this picture with a series he was collecting for Japanese military purposes. Rose, he considered, studying the angle of her shoulder and the way her full mouth smiled, would be a valued comfort woman for a senior officer of the East Asia Co-Prosperity zone.

Lover, good-time girl, tart, three angles of the same face, Rose, transposing one over the other, one photograph with no foothold anywhere telling a thousand stories of nothing more than a question, a perhaps.

She found the note, later, folded, under a box she kept for hair pins. The housemaid, she was sure, had put it there. It was the considerate action of someone young, mad for love, fearful of judgement, free of dispensing it.

Yokota Ryuichi looked at her through the eye of his lens. Not once did he look at her to see her as she was. He studied negatives of her dancing in the developing fluid that he pegged to a line to dry.

He had photographs of her in groups, snapped playing a giggling set of doubles at the tennis club, and after the game, too, hugging her drink and rolling her eyes round to peer up at soldiers. Sometimes Yokkie, as he was popularly known, took shots of her at the department store, Whiteways, in the company of women at morning tea. Dressed in their pretty floral dresses, mittens, straw hats and bouquets, they gathered to admire a new Wedgwood table setting, the pink napkins winged like butterflies between a carefully selected silver service. In the afternoons, he would photograph the same women tittering over drinks at fashion parades or on lawns where bands played the latest music, events staged by Penang's better hotels.

An older woman who smiled in the vacuous manner of the inebriated accompanied Rose on these occasions. Aunt Margaret, a wispy woman dressed crisply in linens, fine muslin, voile, georgette, unlike most of the other women who favoured the island's home dressmaking style of frocks cut from cheap shilling patterns. On one memorable occasion, she wore a linen lace of great beauty, Yokkie noted scientifically in a specifically assigned notebook. A stylish woman, he discovered, with a drinking problem.

Rose dressed to conform to local habits. Her body was young enough to mould a badly cut seam into a better line. He saw her smoke Players cigarettes, drink sherry and lean too heavily against a table scattered with cigarette buts soaking up spilled flowers.

Aunt Margaret, he learned from an assistant at Whiteways, placed special orders for underwear — they used to call it lingerie — favouring oyster silk and lace from Paris, garments whose supply the war in Europe had interrupted. She did not like the more readily available Dorothy More type. And she did not always accompany her niece to the many dances .

There were many dances, cabarets, parties, and balls. It was as if the official military voice reassuring the population that they were safe from menace stirred a frenzied energy overshadowed by a dark foreboding. And they danced. Under tropical moons, through nights scented with frangipanni, round coconut palm, between bouganvillea strung with cardboard stars, they danced with the feverishness of the doomed at the tennis and swimming clubs.

On the dance floors of the hotels, Yokkie photographed Rose spinning with the increasing numbers of young men in uniform the Federated Malay States were welcoming in the late days of September 1941. They were easily found putting a brave face on things, elbowing the bar at the E & O. Some wandered, sadly withdrawn, round the *pasar malam*, not seeing the goods for sale or hearing the hawkers calling the quality and the price of their wares. Others broke through the anxiety stirring their guts by carousing at the club house at Tanjong Tokong, ready and willing, with big easy smiles, swinging rhythmically to match the dancing steps of friendly young women.

Yokkie had no care to understand the unreal situation the British found themselves in. Their homeland was being battered from the air by German forces. He was more alert to the success of the army of his nation that was in Burma and Indo-China.

As new international power-brokers, the Japanese were considered full of cheek and unpredictable. Their military craft had yet to be tested.

Yokkie was aware that the people of Penang who read the newspapers and listened to the news on the wireless and watched the newsreels at the picture houses hoped fervently there would be no war. They hoped with the fervour of those who believed, despite all the signs to the contrary, that no war would shatter their complacency. When military preparations intensified, headiness overwhelmed them. And the newspapers reported in the social pages that the cracklingly fit and smart boys from the airbase danced with a bevy of attractive and cheerfully disposed young women after playing a decent game of rugby against the equally fit and smart navy boys. When attack looked inevitable, the tempo of the music swung more recklessly, the dancing under star-lit skies swirled more frenetically, the columns of engagements' notices spread across several pages in the newspapers, and the numbers of couples hastily taking marriage vows increased.

If we trust the cineaste's picturing of those months before the outbreak of hostilities shook the archipelago, flirtation and fox-trots and falling madly in love — in short, whooping it up — was how it was. Those faces that sink behind cameras to look at the world through lenses, failing to imagine life and its complexities, see only the framed simplicities they choose above others to value.

In rooms heavy with sweat dampening sweetly perfumed powders and eau-de-colognes, Yokkie's camera may have captured a melancholy swelling Rose's bottom lip. Occasionally, she would sway tearfully to a voice-over crooning Al Bowlly's love-lorn lyrics. But his camera, catching her draining her glass, did not see she hid a mournfulness behind a mouthful of gin and tonic. In the frames he developed, he saw a spirited young woman throwing back her head, exposing her throat, her body moving to the imitated strains of the Ray Noble band under a variety of tropical moons.

Yokkie had no imagination for this game Rose swung into, apparently for fun. He judged her sternly. He had no criteria for measuring her way of playing not entirely in a dissolute fashion for future stakes. He aimed his camera at her at the Botanical Gardens and at Tanjong Bungah picnicking by the sea with an Australian soldier who, in civilian life before signing on, had been an engineer with United Engineers. In fact, Rose spent most of her daytime hours during a few weeks in October 1941 standing in a back room with her arms above her head, slowly turning on a table for the dressmaker to fit the new frocks she ordered to wear when she went out with Russell Wild.

Russell worked in radio communications. He wanted Rose to go with him to Ceylon before he had to 'bunk off' on a secret assignment. He thought Ceylon would be safer than Penang and more to her liking than Australia. He told her there would be a scuffle with the Japanese, and that she should leave while the going was good and be with him in Ceylon which was, he said, "First-rate. First-rate place. Lots of sea and palm trees. And plenty of good food to eat."

Russell Wild said he wanted to marry Rose.

On the sands of Tanjong Bungah where sweet smelling jungle flowers perfumed sea air, Rose hesitated before a few confused presentiments of her future. Russell was ardent. His ardency forewarned her he may not take kindly to discovering she was no virgin. In the England she had come from, the long shadow of Queen Victoria may not have bothered the middle upper middle or middle middle upper or lower middle middle upper class she came from. Rose had observed Australians, on several questions of morality, lacked a kind of sensibility she took for granted. Mateship bonded men, and women were mateship's outsiders. There were no tacitly understood social rules presupposing delicacy, some would say deviousness, in personal matters. Apart from a violent dislike of authority, Australians, according to Rose's observations, were emotional drifters freely dependent on their own whim. Sentimentality, a violence in itself, governed individual passion or group indifference.

This, she noticed, made some of the men crude. Others like Russell Wild were possessed of a personal dignity. Rose thought he was considerate. Gentle. A bit bland, perhaps. Rose had no illusions about how her life would be with Russell Wild.

Shrewdly calculating the depth of his simplicity, she told him a plausible story about an Englishman she loved. She said he was a long-loved somebody who returned to England with the promise he would announce their engagement and send for her to follow him, and they were to marry. "But he hasn't written." Sobbing quietly, she confided, "I have an awful feeling he's lost his life. Blitz, you know. The blitz." It was the sort of story an ardent romantic like Russell Wild would want to believe. Unsettled times improved its veracity.

Fixed in a triptych, Rose, the good time girl who might become a Japanese officer's comfort woman became a soldier's fiancée anticipating a feckless life in Colombo. She looked forward to dancing under the fabulous ceiling at the Mount Lavinia Hotel, swimming at Galle and motoring with someone else's husband to drink tea at Kandy. She might just leave behind being a love-sick woman who forgot how long she sat by her bedroom window after dancing till dawn, wondering if the predicted war with the Japanese intercepted her heart's true beat.

In another frame, her future with Wang Li-tsieng held a speculative fascination for which her imagination held no precedence. In the labyrinthine formulation of *baba* families, Li-tsieng's uncles BK and Cho were China educated, more conservative than their eldest Straits educated brother who was Li-tsieng's father. The senior Wang was the Patriarch, responsible for his own household of four wives, several concubines, servants, retainers and his many children as well as his brothers and their households.

Those brothers advised their oldest brother's first born son against socialising with women. They taught the boy Li-tsieng women should be kept in the house as wives and concubines, and that a woman's best company was enjoyed in bed. In his twentieth year when he was so much in love with Rose, Li-tsieng did not have the courage to flout Uncles Cho's and BK's attitudes by disobeying his father's directive to sail to Chile.

Li-tsieng wrote her letters. He sent them to the boy in his pay at the E & O with instructions to give them to Rose, but the boy kept them in a box because he was not sure how to deliver secret love letters to a white woman with a 'reputation' for being 'a naughty miss', 'a saucy wench', 'a good-time girl'. He had seen her dancing with soldiers long past midnight. On moonlit nights on a whitened beach, he had seen her broadened into the concealing bulk of a male body. The black and white landscape spoke a distinctive language. It was like an old movie with its scratching sound played out in Black & White, its message clearer than seeing colours intensified by daylight.

Neither revealed anything of Rose's reality.

A great love, according to Milan Kundera, in his novel, *The Unbearable Lightness Of Being* and many authorities before him, is like the fitting together of fine musical phrases, the lovers complementing each other just so, separable but more resonant, richer in tone and stronger when counterpointed. Orchestral pieces come to mind. Symphonies glance the air with the lyrics underlying the repeated delight the world sees in lovers drinking in each other through liquid eyes. Overlooked, as Kundera reminds us, is the less grand, the popular dance band music of the lovers' generation. Rose, not caring to be symphonic, may have liked herself described as a note falling from a saxophone, waiting to be picked up by a swinging clarinet with drums and piano putting in the jazz beat for a love story told on celluloid.

Al Bowlly, crooning in the shadows for a good many amateur romantics, sugared her heart. She dropped his records on her gramophone, wound the handle and she danced mournfully around the sitting room at Dunn Street like every other star-struck girl, remembering Li-tsieng and thinking very little of Russell Wild as the needle grated over the grooves. Yokkie would have understood this Rose. This Rose, malingering for her love, was his perfect although least useful woman.

For Gillian Hindmarsh, the historian, there is no message on the grainy surface of Yokkie's photograph. A dance may have excited the unknown woman, a man may have pinned a nosegay to her shoulder, they may have touched fingers over cocktails. That life, figured by a dress and a woman's anonymous face, is and is not Gillian's vision of a fabulous past distorted at will. When she stirs the rice frying in a wok on the gas stove in her flat, Gillian stirs through her memory of the mud and the sunshine of life on her family's farm to her lingering desire for sensual laziness. Her desire to gratify the physical senses is similarly shared by Patrick Dreher and Badul Mukhapadai who both long for it in the form of a slower pace accompanying a simple innocence, which Shi-zheng intends to demolish.

But Gillian is at cross-purposes with herself. The photographed face at the centre of her obsession may be exotic. It may express an old-fashioned way of being a woman that criss-crosses the neurotic romance Gillian desperately seeks and equally as desperately rejects. The face, the light glancing off the tooth, the tips of the pointed eyes, begs the questions Gillian has read in books and has seen projected on the screen about the illusory life lived by a few before the Second World War. Ideologically, the photograph is telling a story Gillian impatiently dismisses. The historian sees nothing in it but sentimentality, a motherhood issue of history. She is not interested in biographies hinting at the last three months of a life when circumstance wrested itself from fate. Rather, Gillian prepares to tolerate a reading of her own situation under the same heading, calling it by its other name, destiny. She is a blunt piece of work, throwing up her breakfast and worrying about the lateness of her period. Her life, conventional thus naturally real, was unguarded when the condom slipped off in a heated moment with her young lover, Patrick.

Gillian is not fascinated by the fears daunting those people who 'didn't make it', the ones who left their leave-taking from Penang too late to gain safe custody in Australia, Ceylon or Africa. It is of little interest to her, not worthy of a sneer, that Rose's uncle accepted it was incumbent on him to organise a passage to a 'safe haven' for 'his women' and himself. She did not care at all that Cedric Willoughby suffered an emasculating powerlessness in the face of the events he predicted.

Cedric saw 'his women' were increasingly disturbed, but a labour problem at Ipoh unsettled the tin mining operations of his company. When he got around to booking a passage to Ceylon, that is to say, looking after 'his women', Uncle Cedric Willoughby was surprised he could not secure cabins on any ship sailing to Colombo before December 9.

He excused himself. He was uncommonly burdened. Cedric Willoughby, and only Cedric Willoughby, had to settle that problem at Ipoh. It assumed greater and greater importance as the plausible reason for not leaving as the days sped by.

He knew Rose mooned and danced and played records and disappeared at night until the early hours of the following morning, but he had no energy to 'put his foot down and put a stop to' her wilful behaviour. He saw her reading the long letters Russell Wild wrote, and this pleased him because, he thought, that was a 'good lad', 'right for her'. But he frowned when he saw the pages strewn around the sitting room, out of order and not read twice. It was as if she were discarding the writer himself. Despite her uncle advising, with a lot of muttering and harumphing "Russell Wild. Fine fellow," Rose looked doubtful. And Cedric Willoughby was not one to push a girl. "If you so choose," he growled one day at breakfast over marmalade and toast, "you ... War, you know, Rose. Must think ahead. Stay safe. And you. You may like to stay with your Aunt Margaret. And mysel'." He cleared his throat noisily, making way for a deepened voice grating over a throat unused to words expressing how he felt. "I quite like having you around, Rose." Covering his mouth with his napkin, he hastily explained, "...eer, booked. All for all three of us to sail for Colombo. All three of us."

"First available passage," he coughed. "No point hanging around," he said. "Looks all set to go."

Aunt Margaret forgot Uncle Cedric said they were headed for Ceylon. Weeping whenever a letter bearing an English postage stamp arrived, she hoped to join her family at the Orchard Cottage, Little Chart, to which they evacuated in 1940. She read and reread of a cousin's child's wedding at the church at All Hallows, Barking-at-the-Towers, then she set to celebrating the event with many gins. Aunt Margaret's drinking, part of her family's composite picture of itself, had become hazardous.

Arranged in a wicker chair in light coloured, soft materials, Aunt Margaret rocked, shedding streams of silent tears. Prescient, her saturated mind was numbed by a featureless dark. She did not know where she was or where she might sail, or what lay in between here and there. As it was, and Gillian never overlooked the fact, ships were bombed and survivors were either killed or imprisoned. Many were executed later, or died of starvation, beatings, sicknesses.

Being caught up with her difficulties, Gillian has no space in her brain for imagining anything other than a stereotype to explain the life of Rose and Margaret, which she would censure. And whether she knew her time and place in history lacked value or not did not dissuade Rose. Ceylon, South Africa, Australia, what it did it matter? All three looked promising. The prospect of swinging through the war years with lots of young men then returning with Russell to Australia, or another if Russell Wild did not survive the theatre of war engaging his expertise, induced in her a kind of inertia.

Becalmed in marriage, Rose may have become a suburban myth, a wickedly charming woman with a gimlet eye for the men who crowded around to light her cigarette and fetch her another martini and dry. If there were children, she would neglect them as people and love them as others do their puppy dogs. If one refused her ingratiation and snapped at her, Rose would hand it to its father 'to do something serious, darling'. If there were granddaughters, Rose would enjoy polluting their minds with adages about the virtues of flirting. She might instruct them in how to catch a man and make him a husband, a necessity in life rather like a bank account. Certainly, she would quote the axiom 'Better that he should love you more than you love him.' After another martini or two, she would repeat herself, saying, 'It's better that a man should love you more than you love him.' To which she would add, 'That way, you avoid being taken for granted.'

Her granddaughters, watching for her eyes to pop wide open in the same moment she popped the olive into her mouth and dropped her eyelids coyly with this wisdom, would chorus, "Get Real, Gran'ma!" Embracing all the realities, Rose's granddaughters would most likely study relationships therapy and business management, and how to avoid AIDS while having a good time in the stainless steel cities of the postmodern world.

As it was, fate grasped the disorderly moment proffered by war. Willy nilly, Uncle Cedric was unable to understand why he dithered at the brink of a catastrophe. He rightly nursed a concern for Rose. Unknown to him, she had given up any thought of living the routine life of matrimony and enjoying suburban granddaughters with Russell Wild. She was desperately hopeful Li-tsieng would meet her, in body or soul hardly mattered to her. Margaret was a soak, and Ipoh was beset with the jitters. So it was that the Willoughby's suffered the indignity of crowding onto whatever deck space they could find when they left Penang without Rose on December 10.

Even if Rose had gone with her aunt and uncle on the passage booked for Ceylon on December 9, she would have died.

Uncle Cedric was able to survive the sea and the camps. After the war when his skeletal body wandered up the crazy path at Orchard Cottage for a cup of tea — "Lardy cake! Not had in Years!" — he tearfully told the family in England the story of Rose going missing and of the bombing and Margaret's drowning. The medical people had advised him not to rush at food. Taking the teacake between fingers trembling with joy and caution, he neglected to fill in the indelicate detail of his wife's drunkenness at the time of the hit. No need, really. Everyone guessed, and some of the more impressionable nieces and nephews had a fleeting image of their aunt happily tossing over waves she believed were part of a sea filled with gin. They gave the memory of Margaret a life. But they had no imagination for Rose.

Drifting at the edges of Aunt Margaret's misery before the fateful voyage, Rose, with an ancient patience she would never have believed she was capable of possessing, waited for news of Li-tsieng. As if there was a mark on her forehead saying that's how it would be, a lassitude weighed down her limbs, and she could not do otherwise.

Gillian, in 1982, her head aching and her breasts unmistakably too tender to touch, bridles at the thought of marrying. Staring into the porcelain toilet bowl in the damp hours before dawn, Gillian tries looking past her discomfort at plans to guarantee a settled life with her child. She grimaces from the pain of freezing her love of Patrick into ice cubes, easier to box into memory as an interlude, and she worries about a persistent longing for a permanent companion.

And so it is, on the evening before she arranges to leave Penang, Gillian is content to sit in the old house on Jalan Dunn. Not a breath stirs. Meena's family are unusually silent, their high pitched Tamil quiet for the while, and she drinks in something of the beauty the island was once able to share with those of a slower period in history who stopped to open their senses, merge, as Yokkie's camera may have misrecorded Rose doing, into the surroundings, into the scent of frangipannis. Together, Patrick and Gillian hear the low hum of an occasional car, the call of the hawkers selling curry puffs and *nyonya* cakes, the clacking sticks announcing vendors of dubious ice cream and the swishing rubber tyres of the rickshaws. Folding her hands over her over-active stomach, forestalling a violent retching, Gillian rocks backwards into Patrick's arms. She lets free her personality to heave upwards and shed itself of conspicuous meaning.

Traversing another set of dynamics, Gillian gropes between old and new ways of thinking. She closes her eyes, and she hears her voice slip over the silence, not as an interloper, but as something belonging to the house and the neglected compound. She smokily tells Patrick that she is pregnant with his child, and she will have the baby to keep. Her voice rides on its own weariness, insisting that it is her right to allow him to enjoy fatherhood, too, but only during school holidays. Gillian expounds her belief in motherhood independent of fatherhood. To her sudden surprise, she feels Patrick's body stiffen and pause and shake and burst with tumultuous emotions leaping over the infringements she places on him. He smothers her with kisses and carresses. And Gillian, in the way of pregnant women radiating the deepest calm, is open enough for the briefest moment to be held fast by something close to joy.

♓

11. at the way station

What stammers alive to wake the world up?
 Two fishes intertwine to look back at Gillian, but what of Rose basking by the moon's light in a big man's embrace?
 She sat on a beach, perhaps it was Tanjong Bungah. Or was it at Tanjong Tokong that she waited for dawn? There was a whispering blackness, a slow crashing gathering into silences.
 Sea.
 Like a lake.
 She heard herself breathing.

Rose breathes into Gillian's sleep. Between gloved fingers, she balances a cigarette holder. A saxophone's trailing note winds round a pale moon. Her gloved finger taps the cigarette holder. Ash drifts thinly.
 Gillian, slipping through moon beams, slides over the photograph of a young woman, and pleats herself into the decade preceding her birth. Slinkily dressed in an evening gown that has an orchid pinned to its shoulder strap, Gillian assumes the staged presence of Bette Davis. She becomes Rose.
 Waiting.
 Waiting for who, waiting for what?
 Doors bang. A tale crackles with the music scratching a record wobbling under the heavy needle arm of an old gramophone.
 At the end of a corridor, the tip of a cigarillo glows.
 Time snaps an arm, a record flies round a room, photographs buckle. A Black & White movie spins through a life.
 What is it?
 Gillian's eyes hunt the dark.

Shadows lurking at her bedroom's edges snicker and wheeze and sink down where dreams squirm. Their serpentine writhings squeeze under the large wardrobes and the rattan chairs and tables.

She cannot escape the dreamt life. An energy swings the floor from under her. She skids, swinging as if she is a puppet, ungainly without its strings.

Someone has waited too long.

"Passing up, passing by alternatives, making do with an imitation," a voice whispers. "Are you that?"

A voice whispers, "Gillian!"

Gillian, sheets twisted round her hips, sits up straight. A smooth skinned young man sleeps with his hand curved like an unopened lotus by her hip. Patrick, a Bogart hat shadowing his face, is sitting at the end of the bed. He is dressed for a European winter, a grey woollen overcoat amply folding round his body, and he flicks the air with black leather gloves.

"Is he the original?" Patrick's voice is low.

He begins to say, slapping his gloves into the palm of his hand, "I have a right to ask." Then he looks straight at her and he says, "Rightly or wrongly, you're the only person I've ever loved. Rightly or wrongly, I believe I have a right to know that everything is best for you."

A balloon puffs up above her. Empty of words, it sways.

Gillian finds herself gasping, frighteningly awake in the dark of her room where shadows slide down the walls and flicker across the ceiling. She lies still. Her heart pounds so hard her breastbone shudders. It is a still night. A dream, something about Patrick, slithers from the edge of her memory. A single shout of horror, as if someone has seen a ghost, reels through the dark.

She listens more carefully.

She hears herself breathing.

It is her tenacity that surprises Gillian Hindmarsh.

When she is preparing to leave Penang, Gillian finds herself astride a banking moment. As an historian, she is afraid of a sensation of being tossed aside, even cast adrift, by the big events in time contradicting another sensation. Or does a primeval voice scream through her heart? Does its shrill insistence, that she will give blood to the life quickening inside her and quite a good deal of her love, drive the contradictory currents of her mood?

Filling out slips of paper and waiting to hear her name called, the pregnant Gillian is filled with dreaminess. She dreams of rushing to catch buses, trains, airplanes. She thinks over her nightdreams, and redreams the parts where she is forever waiting, waiting to embark on a dash through the unknown landscape of destiny, fast.

On a train.

It is a train that stops in her nightdreams.

The train stops for her to embark on the top of a hill. It chugs to the end of the platform. It shunts down a difficult descent. But mud slides across the tracks, toppling the engine, pushing over the carriages, and sections of track spear the air. There is no vista, no breathtaking dawn greeted from the train window, no golden rainwashed day breaking over low-lying hills. There is none of the silent wonder of a dreamer facing the back of the dreamself's head that steadily blocks the emptiness of a window opening on such a world. In her nightmare, Gillian's dreamself struggles up an unsealed road to the station. She sits on the platform to wait for the train. The train chugs to the end of the platform. It shunts down a difficult descent. Mud slides across the tracks. The engine topples. Carriages spill. Sections of track spear nothing. Gillian rescues her bags. She drags herself up the slippery road to the station. She needs a new transport. She needs a new landscape. She needs a new focus.

If this were a movie, it would be no Black & White drama with Gillian cast as Bette Davis acting the feminine lead. Nor would it be a moody art piece with Gillian, dreary and encumbered in skirts, wheezing painfully at the awfulness hounding her heavy steps. No. Gillian's panoramic dreamscapes are clearly parchment green dominated by a zany blue sky, the houses glittering red brick squares. And the music. If she had her choice, Gillian would have a thousand violins rustling through treetops, her struggles in old jeans and a shapeless T-shirt repeated. Violins, playing a music that vibrates with zephyrs at dawn, was the music to accompany her repeated climb to the station on the hill top.

Hearing no rooty tune or spirited chamber music, nor anything symphonic, she may be the silent endurance that characterises too much in women's history. The dreary resonance repeats itself. From her grandmothers down the ages to herself, Gillian struggles up the steep hill of destined life, and, like them, she is always alone. The tedium is for her, and her alone.

If a cineaste follows this nightmare as an action filmed for the cinema, Gillian may be angled against the odds, her unpainted face refusing to be looked at and appraised. Is she a doughty woman 'getting on with it', not pausing to wonder what the hell the 'it' might be? Maybe she is playing at being an Earth Mother who chooses her fate.

Is she an enigma refusing to sit still at the station?

Gillian wants to leave the lonely station. Balancing her lack of an elegant cigarette holder against her desire to hold the baby, she paces the length of the platform. Her future as a mother with a higher degree in history is ahead of her, and she will strive to take the high ground. Nevertheless, in her nightmare, she is on the old route. Motherhood is the old route invading her dreamspace. Re-establishing the parameters, Gillian is daring to look away from being looked at.

She steps through the carriage door. She sits by a window. She waves goodbye. The engine hoots and chugs to the end of the platform. It shunts down the steep hill and topples in a mudslide. Carriages spill. Sections of track point skywards. Perhaps her dreamself, slipping in mud, is fearful she is to remain like all the full-skirted and blue-jeaned women the world over, repeatedly struggling up the old road under the weight of bags. Bags and babies. But the wide-awake Gillian, wanting everything, expects herself to be self-sufficient, sharing none of the responsibility, nor any of the love, of her child.

"Women," she dictates to Patrick, perhaps tyrannically when he pleads with her to marry him, "must face their destiny alone."

But in this moment, she is in the bank where a teller walks across the room to touch her shoulder. She pushes back her hair, and finds herself peering at the benign face of a bespectacled middle-aged man who is explaining her documents are ready for signing.

She follows the teller. In her head, she is stepping away from a railway station where hapless trains pause before losing themselves in a hillside village sliding into mud. Gillian gathers the metaphor that stylises women's history to examine it for thought as surely as she gathers her financial documents to peruse and then sign. Flourishing her fountain pen, she questions how circular is this history, that long thought careless of women, and she finds it is more like opinion, more like unquestioned habits. Tradition, that is to say.

The teller politely asks when her husband will be able to endorse her documents. Stunned that she should hear such a question, Gillian thwacks her passport on the desk, declaring "There never was one." The teller withdraws, apologising for 'a slip of the tongue, Madam', 'a habit of thought', and for the island's conservative ways.

Turning her head away from him, she looks through the glass partitions where she sees a woman tourist waiting while her male partner cashes travellers' cheques. Gillian felt threatened, a post-modern woman who was determined to be responsible for herself. She wished she had the elan of Bette Davis, elegant in her anger, thus effectively powerful in the culture around her.

On Weld Quay, there was a Railway Pier. No train ever pulled through its yards. It stood at the end and at the beginning of a ferry ride from the railway station on the mainland to the ferry terminus on the island and back again. Its edifice was grand. Bombs consigned it to the glorious museum of architectural history, an example of evolving styles and other ways of moving people from a point of departure to a place of destination.

Railway House survived the war. In 1982, it houses Customs and Immigration offices. Near it, inside the Ferry Terminal and under its high ceilings, cars groan. Petrol stinks the air. Large metal girders ride across each other and clang together. Greased ropes tug tight. The links of large chains bite into each other. The ferryman collects coins for the journey to the railway station on the mainland and, in 1982, a bridge is being built to take the increased flow of traffic, also answering the modern demand for speed. The toll for crossing by bridge will be paid in paper money.

Gillian, studying pre-war documents, may ponder the strangeness of the Railway Pier and its less than grand descendant, the Ferry Terminal. If she found the building plans for the Pier's construction, she would examine the details and the features closely, studying the Victorian marriage with Saracen influences that melded in a particular way in India to produce an ornate Edwardianism.

There, too, is the significance of an island serviced by a railway that bore no trains, an island constantly departed from for another embarkation point, the farewell from the station platform diminished by the farewell from the ornate Pier. The island, the point of arrival for seafarers, was the point of departure for the ferry passengers, their destination the platform in a muddy village across the water.

When the calligraphic characters inked onto the document in front of her sprawled weakly under an early morning wave of nausea, Gillian may steer away from this idea.

Penang itself is, for her, a loved place. Penang would be the final destination, and not the departure point, surely, for many.

Studying the decorative exteriors and functional interiors of public buildings is her preferred way of seeing the world. By restricting the possibility of introspection in her research, she has no fear of being unsettled by sightings of herself. She does not care a whisker about the people massing at the modern Ferry Terminal, their destination a railway station. It could be said they are at the beginning of a journey which is an end, circling, never arriving, like history itself. Or is this Ferry Terminal the way station where overburdened women clamour to find a passage to the mainland, little realising they must travel light, unencumbered by a lot of old bags if they expect anything like independence?

Are women to be left behind, stranded on the side of the road, on the quay, on the railway siding — with the baby and the requisite bags?

Gillian has no picture of herself dwarfed by the ornate British colonial Railway Pier or the Malaysian Ferry Terminal preceding the watery journey to a railway platform. Although she spends her days studying the plans for buildings like the old Pier, her sub-conscious focus takes for destiny's landscape her agrarian past, the train in her dream forever skidding down the hill of a rude village on the eastern seaboard of Australia.

Is the village on the hill representing the grip the past holds over her, strangling the present with odium? What is this past?

Wang Shi-zheng, opening the door of his Mercedes on Beach Street where the banks are, almost knocks over the running figure of a European woman. He steps back, shocked by her strength and speed. Shocked, too, by her terrible ungraciousness. He recognises who she is, the historian, what's-her-name? He may never have been told. He has no name popping up in his head. He steps away from his car, and he carefully closes its door as he adjusts the information that the fast running woman is the friend of Patrick Dreher, a tenant in a Wang house and a dredging engineer working for Dutch-Malaysian-Korean interests.

Gillian, whipping down the street and round the corner, is coddling a memory of future bliss drawn from the remembered smell of a friend's baby. She is going back home. To her mother. To give birth. To get a grip on her future.

Perhaps.

Perhaps, in order to manage her pregnancy alone, Gillian is revisiting her home where her mother, who would ply both needle and thread to fill cupboards with baby clothes and bed linen, lives out her days. But Gillian cannot repeat her mother. She has done something to the way she thinks, severing herself from the continued description of women as creatures biologically designed to carry embryos, remaining embryonic themselves, in rooms shared with others, under clocks telling the time quartered for the advantage of others. Gillian will neither hang around gazing at vistas in the hope she might catch sight of salvation, nor live a life fatalistically anticipating a reincarnation into a better one. Here, in the present continuously evolving into the future that dissolves into the present, Gillian will adapt to become a new construction of herself, developing her self-sufficiency. Urgently. She possesses no memory of her future as a single mother.

Gillian's dreamself turns her back on the hilly railway station. She goes to the plains of grass on the outskirts of the village where she will find an airfield. In her day-to-day real world, she will go to the plains where grass once grew at Bayan Lepas. It is the airport on the island of Penang. The plane, taking her in its uterine belly up from one port and down to another, will fly her back home where, six months hence, her baby will be born.

The image of a red-faced European woman running at the opening door of his car drops from Wang Shi-zheng's brain.

After all, he is concentrating on share-trading. He is playing the Bourse in futures.

Rose knew none of these adages about women facing their destiny alone. She read no history. She read nothing about the many cultures and religions of Asia. She was ignorant of Vedic or other truths pinning multitudes of women under single words and those axioms signifying despair was their lot if compliance was not complete.

For her, days happened much like any other. Rose, seated on a sofa or walking round the living room, ran her fingers over silver ashtrays, and opened and shut Aunt Margaret's silver and shagreen cigarette box lying under an alabaster table lamp. The silver inlaid on the grainy texture of the untanned leather under her fingers reassured her that life was real enough to be touched. Spinning the wheel of her own silver lighter, she watched the flame burst straight up. Rose waited. When she waited, at first for the hour to leave on an errand that was not an errand at all but an assignation, later in October and November, for a few words, Rose dropped a record on the gramophone, lowered the needle arm and wound the handle. Her heart fluttered for a note, or any news at all. She waited, her melancholy softening her red lips pouting through pleated drapes.

In this, she was beautiful, having the vitality of still movement. Like fish between reeds.

Like snow melting in a silver bowl.

Rose faced her fate alone.

When she walked with Aunt Margaret in the company of women through the Waterfall Gardens, Rose joined some of the other younger women, as a formality, being their age herself. Romanticisms like apparitions and reading tea leaves and the astrologer's charts were discussed as if they were a science, these young women quoting them as guidelines on which they should pin their hopes. What if one of them read her morning teacup with an intelligent eye on the future? Rose giggled with them about the strange fates that might befall them.

"We'll all be doomed!"
"Married! With children!"
"Oh no! Not that!"
"Doomed!"
"Lots of smelly socks in the wash!"
"Alas!"

What a giggly girly lot they were!

They spread a rug over the soft grassed mound where a band sometimes played. Rose sat to one side of a Cissy or a May, perhaps a Julia, listening to their long pattering about every article of clothing ever worn — the advantages of silk over lisle stockings, colours of lipsticks one might choose, whether rouge on cheeks became a girl or made her look a tart, and how to preserve a fresh look at dances despite the humidity and the closeness of the atmosphere. One servant made tea in a fine silver pot from hot water carried in a large thermos. Another spread across the plaid rug trays of dainty cakes and sardine sandwiches. The women freely shared the advice, with much animation, that one had simply to mash the tinned fish with pepper and a hint of lime juice, a recipe read in the women's pages of the *Singapore Herald*.

The women, Aunt Margaret and the mothers of Cissy and May, prattled on about dinners and parties they had been to. They talked endlessly about the strange sighting at six in the evening of a wayward young man hovering around a wayward young woman's window, a uniformed nurse and a new kind of woman to Penang. Sometimes Cissy's mother would exchange glances with May's mother. Neither wished to be rude. Neither wanted to disturb the apparent tranquillity of mind Margaret Willoughby was blessed with, informing her of all the scrappy stories about Rose and her mid-afternoon flits around the Beach Street area before suddenly heading straight for the E & O. Worse! The gossips spread all over town that, since September when the object of her fascinations had left Penang, she danced and stayed out late with 'all sorts'!

If Rose was framed by any reality at all, she would be bordered by these neat white sandwiches and dainty cakes packed in pink linen napkins, the servant smiling, lifting the tea service to replenish the fine bone china cups especially reserved for picnics. The young women sat prettily in wide brimmed straw hats, hair softly curling on their shoulders. Gathering floral skirts round their sandals, the older women sat on small picnic chairs. Yawning, and sipping a third or fourth cup of tea, having nothing left to say, they dozed.

Aunt Margaret slyly pressed something pewter to her lips. After a few minutes, her eyes watchful, she pressed the something to her lips for a longer moment. She lowered it, slipped it into her handbag, and resumed her blissful contemplation of the ferns.

Rose saw her but Rose never thought to question her Aunt Margaret or judge her drinking as a fall from grace. When she was sent by her aunts and uncles in England to Penang to find a husband, she was pleasantly gratified by Aunt Margaret's lack of stridency. Rose was not hindered by any personal guilt about her love affair. Worried by a late period, she was surprised when Aunt Margaret told her, quite unprompted, there were ways not to have children. For her, Margaret Willoughby, having periods and no children was the worse problem. Consequently, Rose felt confident that if she was pregnant, Aunt Margaret would love her more rather than less, for wanting to be alive.

There was, too, so much shared warmth with her, of not saying very much, of lazily being in her dotty company.

Even so, Rose quietly asked Meena's mother how to bring on her period. Not backward at ensuring she should make a brew that was both effective and punishing, the housekeeper put her knowledge to work. The purgative left Rose weakened for ten days. But she was strong enough. Meena's mother's raised eyebrows judged that this one was a candidate for this punishment many more times.

Rose had kept her 'women's problems' secret from Li-tsieng. From the little she knew of the ways of the *baba* families, if he knew she was pregnant, he would want to make her his second wife, a position in life she was not prepared to endure. She loved the room in the E & O he frequently filled with yellow roses for her. She loved the game of shadows she played with the hibiscus when she left him in the afternoon. She loved slipping away from dances to meet him there. Knowing he was not hindered by his sexual life being described as illicit, Rose had no illusions. And she had no desire to be his wife left in the luxury of the family mansion, waiting for him to come back to her from assignations such as these she herself enjoyed so much.

October, 1941. And no note. Nothing bearing Chilean postage stamps found its way into her hand.

May and Cissy were discussing the program at the picture house. Their hands flitted over the grass and smoothed their skirts. Their lips moved rapidly from laughter to smiles to discussing hypothetically the intimacies a movie star's life might possess. When their mothers and Aunt Margaret looked to be sleeping, Cissy whispered she had met a special man, "Navy!" Her fingertips walked on air and her eyelashes were beaded with excited tears, and deliciously she asked, "Is anyone able to cover for me if at the dance on Friday, I …" Her face shone. Rose smiled. May giggled and frowned and warned and prevaricated and, after a lot of frantically whispered coaxing, she agreed to cover for Cissy by saying she was at the tennis club and not at the dance when she would really be meeting her young man at a bungalow at Tanjong Tokong.

In any case, the teacup readings pointed to a moonfull of Mr Right for Cissy.

With them, Rose was and will be alone. When she listened

to their giggles and Cissy's plans, she felt old. She liked them, both of them, and she had no need of them. Looking askance, she did not ask, "Why, May, would you hesitate to help Cissy meet her Mr Right?"

These pretty faced young women, fair and freckle skinned under their large straw hats, had only one memory of the future, as wives and mothers, best surrounded by a good garden and a well-established house. How could any one of them have a memory of the future that was approaching through the jungles?

What of Cissy's teacup, with its prediction of Mr Right? Would the leaves have formed a pattern telling she would follow her father, leaving with her family for Singapore, by the end of the month? Would any patterning have shown her immediate future working with her mother as a volunteer nurse at Gleneagles in Singapore?

Poor Cissy. Will she peel back skin burned with cloth to see the disfigurements of war too soon and too often after declaring her love with promises of a life filled with rosy pink hope in the bungalow at Tanjong Tokong? Was there written in her teacup how a quiet-mannered doctor raised his black eyebrows and steadied his brown hand and steeled his anger, his bewilderment? There was no legal escape for an able-bodied man, no alternative for a doctor but duty, and he was Eurasian with no way out of an inferno with worse to come. Perhaps the teacup saw his name, John van Cuylenberg, whose book, *Singapore Through Sunshine and Shadow*, was published posthumously. But the teacup failed to tell how his story intersected hers. He ordered Cissy's mother, if she loved her daughter at all, to get her on a ship, any ship, and out of Singapore during that mad week in February, 1942. One thing is sure. Cissy will know, in the nightmares shuddering the rest of her life, that this world is uncaring of the fragilities marking some of humankind.

May will fare, some would say better, some would say more sadly. Her family will evacuate Penang for Medan where the Dutch authorities, not knowing whose side they were on, stood in the way of their access to boats and papers and information. Late one night, May's mother and father, her two younger sisters and herself, will make their way to Palembang, and the Japanese will capture them. However her story twists, May will survive, and, at the end of the war, a shy note will appear in a newspaper column: *May Wild, nee Reynolds, once of Penang, now of Sydney, would like to receive some news of her relatives. Please write to Box 21, Sunday Times.*

No one will answer her plea.

Grittier, made resilient by war, Russell Wild, her husband, will be her only relative. And perhaps on a summery Sydney evening when the shadows thicken before the sky snaps dark, Russell will hold his beer in a firmer grip, a beach filled with the aromas of jungle flowers beckoning his memory, but he will not give voice to what he is thinking of Penang. And of Rose.

Yes, as it is and as it was, then there is Rose. With Cissy and May. Russell knew all three.

Watching her bags glide through the security screen, Gillian hovers with no ghost attending at the airport. But if she read her teacup, took note of the astrologer's charts, blew a leaf to the wind bearing her dared wish, which one of these would reliably spin the message of her future? What would fish upturn from the grainy bottoms of the ocean for her to consider freshly?

Resigned to the concentricities of his wheeled life, Badul Mukhapadai seeks small respite when he makes love with Mei-mei. But in his dreams, he has been walking with Gillian, a prickly woman whose dreamself carries her sandals in one hand. His dreamself looks across a restless rippling to twin rocks. Tons of water roll and crash. The booming sea in his dream is not the placid Straits. When he wakes, his body sings as if it breathes through all its pores.

Would it be possible, at some future moment, for Gillian to drop on the sand beside him?

Badul rolls to the edge of his bed, pulling his sarong round his thighs, and he remembers the black moment at the close of the dream when the woman's head faces the ground. She studies the sand to see where her feet leave imprints, examining where she has been to assess the path she will follow. Not once does she look at him.

In another dream, Gillian and Badul wander alone and slowly round the deep arc of a dark blue bay. That was Gillian's dream. She tells no one about it.

On the plane, Gillian looks at the photograph of the woman in the slipper satin gown. She looks like Greta Scaachi playing Olivia in *Heat and Dust*. Or was Gillian thinking of Bette Davis standing aloof and looking over her shoulder at the unseen audience of photographs publicising a film whose name Gillian no longer remembered?

Loosened by the excitement of her pregnancy and the news that his wife was pregnant too, Gillian showed Badul the photograph of the woman she had found in the archives. She told him, hoping she did not sound too convinced by the supernatural, how she dreamed about her. "It was the gown, you know. The slipper satin shone in the dream."

Badul, shocked by the photograph, his voice shaking with fear and disbelief, told her the startling story that both he and his wife had dreams about this woman. "In this gown, too." His tone was grave when he said, "Miss Hindmarsh, in our dreams when this woman was rising out of the sea, you were standing on the water's edge, and you were cradling a baby boy, Miss Hindmarsh."

Gillian willed herself to say no more to Badul Mukhapadai who, as if demonically, attracted her. And if her teacup read she would one day hear this man's voice mumbling what may sound like an assurance, an encouragement, followed by the rustling of clothing and some soft grunting, would she take heed of him? There? Under the moon and stars? Riding up the clouds? With fork and knife tearing at an airline chop? What next?

♓

12. *aperçu*

Magic, like the moon, wanes.

There was, on the only bookshelf in the farmhouse she grew up in, an old book called *The Noble Art Of Venerie Or Hunting*. It was a compilation of translations from many European sources about the virtues of hunting and killing with hawks and falcons. The book felt pleasantly soft and raggedy in her hands. Published in London in 1611, the script was Gothic, giving up very little of its meaning to her. And Jacqueline Dark, with no hawk to claw her wrist, disliked the predatory hunter and its sport of killing. But she associated with the book her fondness for her father, for an unearthly aura that seemed to descend like misted cobwebs over the difficulties of his daily life when he took it down to read, with difficulty, a passage or two to her. Although he struggled with the script, her father snuggled in her memory, faintly glowing, venerating the old book in his hands. Just like him to know an obscure English writer like George Turbeville, proving her father, a farmer with a manic depressive wife, that man snuggled in her memory and named, like her, Jack Dark, was an odd ball.

She liked, too, the stories he told about how he came to have that book in his possession. Sometimes he said he bought it during the Second World War when he was stationed in England. He had cycled through Shropshire and Somerset where he said his convict ancestor may have come from. He stopped often to rummage though bookshops, very often buying paperbacks. "War," he said, "is boring. And a paperback fits in a back pocket. Goes everywhere." But when he lifted this one off a bottom shelf at the back of a badly maintained shop in Shropshire, and although he could barely make sense of it, he wanted the book to be his. "Something," he said. "It was something. Connecting. When I held the book, it became something that connected me. To the village." Was he wistful or whimsical when he added, "A place where I may have distant relatives."

Sometimes he said the book was left to him by his mother's grand aunt, a woman, so family legend had it, who arrived in Sydney with a trunk filled with antiques including some books that she proceeded to sell. Then she met a politician who set her up rather well, foreclosing her need to be in any kind of trade.

And there were other stories. One was about a relative who was a thief. There was a bookish aunt who taught Latin at St Hilda's, a Ladies' College at Southport in Queensland. And an uncle who had 'taken to the cloth' and travelled by horseback, baptising babies, muttering wedding words at couples and singing psalms over the buried in the outback. That story claimed the uncle was paid for his services with the book.

Jacq heard all the stories with studious scepticism. What she understood was her father's need to be connected with something other than the vast land they lived in, their green dairy farm so unlike the yellow plains and the red desert immortalised by the myth-makers.

During her university years, when she studied English literature, Jacq wrote stories and poems, some of which were published in small and forgotten literary magazines. Most were about her green and blue beachy Australia. Once she tried to write a short story about her father and his old book about faulconry, but the editor she sent it to did not believe an Australian dairy farmer would know these things. From a street filled with broken iron fences where Jack Dark would never walk, the rejection slip labelled the character 'inauthentic'. 'Too precious'. 'Not credible.'

Sliding the slip back into the envelope with the story, she

recognised with a sinking feeling that characteristic disconnectedness she shared with her father. 'Too precious'. 'Not credible.' Both of them, she concurred, were that. And she understood where the character in her story, said to be her father, was herself, blandness thinly skeining over and holding taut the madness within.

'Inauthentic'.

'Not much good at chops and things.'

What finger flick induced this drifting dreamily when the cat and a spoon and a dish with a moon sprang across a perhaps, wherever that may be?

When Jacq travelled, knotted questions fixed the tourist's naive stare and throttled comprehension. Nothing new added gloss to the already seen which, unquestioned, confirmed simple pictures imply a simple verity. She withdrew to the wakeful dream of visiting those places recognised by their media dominated veneer. From day's end to day's end, bourgeois concerns skewed the mapped way of her seeing.

From the moment she set foot in Jakarta, Jacq felt as if she burst in on something huge. Even at the airport, an odour of despair dampened the already diffident enthusiasm of aggressive young men competing to offer luggage handling services to spongy-eyed travellers. The customs clerk, a Javanese, was not as deferential as the anthropologists famously described him to be. And the taxi drivers were as anonymous, their manner as brusque, as any she encountered in all the other cities of the world she passed through.

Sitting silently at the back of a taxi, she sped to an airconditioned hotel room. Jacq may have seen from her window a family wakening on an island in the swamp between the airport and the city; a golf course where there used to be a copse supporting tribes of monkeys; or a man watching without surprise her taxi race past his ragged bedding sheltered under an expressway interchange. She clearly saw a constant shuffling of the dejected from dry place in the shade to dry place out of the sun. Jacq recognised the despair. She had crossed India, touched base in Harare, and in Sydney she worked as a social worker placing the homeless in emergency housing. She had seen it all before.

Walking into a line of jeeps vying for space with the Mercedes Benzes, the BMWs, the ancient Kingswoods as if the vehicles themselves were phantoms and not the daily traffic groaning from standstill to standstill down a main drag in metropolitan Jakarta, Jacq discovered she competed in a nightmare. The endless shouldering of people in a crowd wearied her. Tired faces loomed. Drained energy ghosted so many brown eyes. Their exhaustion sank under the traffic fumes. Shapes milled through an apricot haze. A small boy's head focussed Jacq's attention momentarily. When a bejewelled woman squawked at her chauffeur, startling Jacq out of sleepwalking, a man bumped her shoulder and lisped softly, "Aah! Lady! Do that again!"

But she was too self-absorbed to be involved in the circus. She had seen it too often on tee vee. Spontaneity tangled up *déjà connu*. Mobility, stilled by a snapshot or added up into fixed concepts for a museum or a docu-drama, reconstructed nothing. Historical settings, sustained or neglected, reflected somebody else's idea of reality, but they were not ever real. Docu-dramas, visuals, and exhibitions in museums lacked the stink of sweating bodies.

After all, some say reality is an ugly thing.

Jacq is real enough.

Jacq, wandering, overlooks an old woman sitting cross-legged beside a few durians, her toothless gums stained with betel juice. The old woman rasps to her companion hawker an untranslatable comment on that white one's unfuckability. The brittle laughter splitting the dusty haziness behind her did not intersect Jacq's trajectory.

Jacq.
Is she a shadow? A cipher? A sighted pogo stick?
She senses a quiet quivering under air.
Therefore, Jacq: A tourist, and not altogether comatose.

A vibrant thrumming hums through bleating car horns and over the sweet and fetid stinks of an unsanitary metropolitan drainage and sewerage system and under the belt of carbon monoxide fumes. At the hovering of midday, Jacq hears trebling quavers not quite lilting under a skinny tree poking an idiot shade over an open drain and an urban rubble designated as a street. Children whip out of a school bus. Hot pink, lurid purple, screaming green school bags zip the sunshine. Taxis and jeeps nose down the narrow street, easing over loose stones and imbedded rocks and outsized potholes. Swiftly and not looking back, the children dart between the vehicles and run from garden gate to garden gate, running on and on and belling into that thing lacking questions. What is it? Complacency? Tradition? Civilisation and all that?

Jacq recognises a question wandering through her head, asking how desperate are the poor of this city.

Caught in the thrall of her own small desperations, Jacq cannot get a grip on the place and learn to know it. She giggles at the sight of a gorgeous transvestite and worries about the young woman with the ancient face who is suckling a baby. Her eyes glaze over when a young man, his face whitened with rice powder and his lips bruised a purplish red, offers to sing while her companion, Bill Berringen, relates self-approving yarns about trade officials and the local business community.

In the bar of their choice, a child slinks up to Bill's shoes to begin cleaning them without asking permission. Which he does not give, spluttering and kicking angrily at the shoe cleaner. The bar owner curtly dismisses the boy. Jacq misses the despair sinking down the face of the boy who subsides under the pale apricot afternoon, his grey clothes a camouflage in Jakarta's chemical air.

When she picks her way through the market in a back street near Bill's house, her body shuddering from the nauseating explosion of smells, she sees the quiet grace of an old mango hawker offering her fruit at a good price. But she does not see the shy curving of the little girls' heads when they smile at a group of men clustering to help her bargain for the mangoes. Nor does she see the filthy but perfectly painted toes of a tiny woman corseted in pleated *batik* and a lace blouse.

Sipping white wine in Sydney and spinning old 78s with Kel, Jacq will retell the letters she writes to him, describing 'the multitudes,' 'the poverty' and 'the fatalism' that made Jakarta the same as Santiago, Bombay, Nairobi.

Aching feet, burned on Jakarta's footpaths, throb under twisted batik. Jacq, opening her eyes in the dark, lies quite still, listening to the quiet thrilling the sweltering night — Jakarta soft footing, sandals brushing dust, a long gasping, a sucking in of breath. Drifting to the edge of answers, she drifts in the greenhouse climate of skin stickily salting skin, of semen clouding the piscine stinks of her own sweating body, the conditions under the batik too dank and humid. When the moment is right, for Jacq panders ridiculously her lovers' comforts, she gently rolls to sit up on her side of the bed.

Leaning into the dark and tilting her head slightly, she sees and searches the sky. For an opening, an *aperçu* if religious, not quite transcendental. Her sleepless body believes it would find a place to retreat into where she should meditate to transform her physical shape to that of a *bodhisattva*, smiling benignly and radiating beatitude as if from a cloud to the end of the edge of the Earth.

She watches one eye follow dust motes through mosquito netted windows. The eye rises upward to look at mould blackening the bricks enclosing the house's compound. A field of bracken ferns grow horizontally on the garden wall. Above the black tentacles soars a pale apricot sky.

The other eye scratches sleep. It slides over a swelling silence. Then both eyes snap wide to hear dawn. Droning. A note dragging a voice. A resonance vibrating the fungal air crying for Allah (praise be). Relishing hope, Jacq crosses her legs. From the lotus, she intones *aum*, opening her body to enhance innocence and embrace a way leading over her passivity to knowledge. Her intoning, foreign to Christianity, somehow muddles the Hindu range with Buddhistic possibilities, and mingles it all with Allah's praises to make of them something else for the greater good that's godliness.

The foul air rippling for the Prophet straightens haphazardly. Several last cries lengthen.

The air in the bedroom seems to stand still.

At the other end of the house, Bill's housekeeper shuffles through a doorway. Cold water, douched down her back, smacks the tiles. The sound of the splashing releases Jacq. Suddenly aware of her body, of her bloodless joints, she curls over her lotus and rolls into bed, clamping her stomach to Bill's back. Lost in the humidity, no, to the unctuosity — whatever! — and so on, her searching losing purpose for not being that.

Is buying things, taking lovers to boast adventure or poking at noodles on famed street corners the way to see the world?

Jacq sees and smells. She gropes sweaty flesh. She stinks of fruit and fish. She buys a set of earrings, a wooden puppet and a broken vase. She may buy cassettes of local music. But in the main she writes and writes on pages and pages of pink, yellow, blue or white airmail paper. With three kisses under her name, she gives her travels to Kel.

Gillian recreates another kind of record from records through which she takes mental journeys.

Gillian does not see irrelevancies. Her mind is orderly. If she wanders down the corridors whose design she has studied, she may clasp her hands on her hips to study a courtyard from a high framed window, but she will not believe she has chanced on a crowd of an earlier decade silently watching fireworks crackling the sky. Gillian's present is not a serial looping of associations. As a conventional realist, she has what is called a clear sharp mind. That may mean she is literally basic.

Nevertheless, her horizons are broadening. Optical fibres will pass into the histories Gillian chooses to acknowledge with grids of information and images touched up to look real enough. Art galleries will exhibit on the computer screen in her study. Illuminated manuscripts and architectural plans described in Jawi and Arabic will open secrets formerly catalogued in dusty archives. And exploring a film set from a fixed perspective gives Gillian the ability to maintain a bloodless distance from her subject, buildings. Freed of dusty cobwebs, sneezing's needless, this simulated travel nicely sweatless. Grotless = Messless.

Travelling from here to there, from there to here, through time and place and neurotic effusion is Gillian's nemesis, pleasuring her with the fear and agony of plunging outside all expectations and beyond herself.

And yet, when she is settling down with her mother and sister, she is one among three women dropping big bottoms onto chairs. They cross long legs and bend elbows and wave long wristed forearms at each other across a cast iron table set down on the pavement outside the coffee shop in Carrington Street, Lismore. Perhaps they are awesome, a cabal of witches stirring froth into the depths of a good coffee. Passing eyes grazing their flesh miss altogther the small details linking one life to another, and the possibility of another yet to be born.

Gillian Hindmarsh is hunching her shoulders. Striving to be rational, she embraces fecundity. Overripe, she shuts her mouth and smiles a lot. But a ghost damns her sleep. Intuition is telling her someone else's mess is becoming hers.

J acq Dark dozes. Her nice enough smile sailing with mangoes drops out of sight when her single snore wakes her up.

♓

13. *all that blue*

The Hindmarsh's farmhouse looks inland, the sea a long way away at its back. It sits up on a breezy summit facing the tops of trees clustered where the byroad twisting through Newrybar forks off the highway. A lot of sky skims their farm's green paddocks. A few Jersey cows left over from a herd of prime butterfat producers lower their rumps to sit under the shade thrown by a windbreak of pine trees. The cows switch their tails at flies irritating their backsides, and they slowly masticate, and bat their long curling eye lashes over their soft brown eyes, blinking at the peace of all that blue.

Lying on a patternless sofa, her skirt rumpled round her waist, Gillian Hindmarsh points her toes up the wall beside the window opening inwardly to the bedroom she shared with Fi when they were little girls. The sisters, lounging on the front verandah of the house, are pleased to know a neighbour's brand new red brick bungalow, perched at the centre of a sun dazzled garden, is out of their line of vision. The sisters, farm girls who moved away from Newrybar to pursue education and take up careers, agree to abhor shining new houses imposed on sylvan tranquillity.

Gillian babbles about Penang and her lover, Patrick Dreher. She is nervously excited, chattily avoiding any mention of pregnancy, apprehensive Fi will find fault with her decision to have the baby. Gillian anticipates a daughter with pleasure. Running her fingers over the cloth of the sofa, searching for the velvet tufts that made up the old floral pattern whorled over springs and kapok, she traces worn-down smoothness.

Fi Hindmarsh, an economist with her own consultancy business in Sydney, has an air of brusque self-satisfaction about her. She slides her bottom up to sit on the broad wooden banisters, leans back against the support pole which thrusts up to the beams exposed under the galvanised iron roof, her eyes wide, perhaps her ears too, as if she is listening for groaning timber — the house sadly needs repair.

Like the cows, Fi drifts into a trance induced by all that blue. For a better view, she raises an arm above her head and hoists one leg up onto the banisters. From this position, she questions Gillian about her career as a university teacher and researcher, abruptly leaping from "How's the writing going?" to "When d'you expect to finish?" Then she drags her eyes away from the blue to take in Gillian. Her older sister is lying on the old sofa, her feet propped up the wall and her skirt frothing round her waist. Fi, puzzled by an attitude of complacence she has not seen before in her sister, directs her next question to her mother, asking "Do you still mean to look after the farm, Mum? Is it getting too much for you?"

Gillian, struggling to find the words to explain she's pregnant, stops pointing her toes at the ceiling to stare at the square of blue surrounding Fi's head. She has been thinking she should not say anything about the ghost of a woman she saw swimming on the floor of the library where she was working on the morning after a particularly memorable evening with Patrick. She should not give that eerie sighting as the explanation for believing she is carrying a daughter. And there was Fi, the daughter who hardly ever bothered to drive north from Sydney to see their mother. She demanded to know what Gillian thought about the well-being of the farm. She wanted it known that she thought Muriel should sell and take herself off to a nursing home or a retirement village. "Pragmatism dictates," she insisted, "that you'd be safer, Mum, in a retirement village. Money-wise, health-wise, company-wise."

Muriel, fingering the cloth of her skirt, falteringly begins to say, "Your father ..." But Fi snaps, "What keeps you here is utterly irrational."

To comfort herself in the face of Fi's rejection of the grey areas of life, Gillian slides her hand over her small stomach. Clearly, Fi was not going to be convinced by any persuasion deriving from an occultist revelation. (In parenthesis it must be said that, when she is delivered of a son, Gillian's faith in the irrational is shaken. And with the wisdom of the new born, the baby will look at her wondering face with unqualified trust, kindling in his mother's body a warmth softening all her reservations about boys. Gillian will call him Leigh.)

But the historian will not eschew her credibility by dwelling on sightings from the spirit world. She is trained to incline her head and raise one eyebrow above an eye that peers along the shaft of her pen at a page of ineffable scratchiness, all the time reminding herself she must never let herself down with regrets and guilty feelings and disappointments. Gillian spends a lot of her time worrying that she must never give into a subliminal fear that she will be sadly alone when she grows older.

Gillian Hindmarsh had not been that way when she left home at the age of seventeen. Then there was a glimpse of someone who was warm with life, and her vitality inspired her younger sister.

In Fi's imagination, big sister Gillian went up the mountains to Armidale and came back strengthened in every way. Big sister was going to be a teacher. Her arms were long and loose, and her neck, thrown back to dramatise a point, looped elegantly. Big sister graduated from Teacher's College with a moderate pass and a lot of energy and a lot of boyfriends. She was almost too excited when she received the notice of her appointment to a small rural school, a two-teacher primary school on the western plains. Little sister Fi had thought, then, optimism made her big sister shine. She had no idea that Gillian was afraid, premonitions about living so far away from the sea stretching into a too real aridity. And yet, when her beautiful big sister came home every fourth Saturday, Fi was aware something sweet in her was drying up.

Gillian admitted to her little sister her far western posting appointment was dispiriting, but she did not say too much about her inability to get along with the people. She did not understand the not-getting-along well enough to talk about it. She described the dusty street and the town's one grocery store, but not the young women who, although no older than she was, were already nursing babies. They stared at her with undisguised hatred for betraying the masochism they believed defined women as the recipients of all humankind's bitterness. And for a girl who had been popular with the boys at Teacher's College, she had no experience with young men who fell silent until she walked by, far enough for her to hear them snickeringly suggest how 'to fuck her stupid like the rest'.

Gillian told Fi most people in the town had nothing to say to anyone who did not drink at the local pub. That included her headmaster. He was an individual of such withering contempt for any enthusiasm, of disgust for any sign of youthful beauty he might see glowing in his classrooms, he hounded it to a far corner to cane it silly.

There was no one for Gillian to confide in about the sadistic headmaster or any of her more personal problems. Her companions were an insufferable clergyman and his wife, a woman best described as dishcloth grey, the mother of their family of six children who all smelt of sour powdered milk and of soap clogged in clothes poorly washed in cold water. Gillian pronounced them "Kind. Enough to invite me to share lamb chops and custard in the middle of the week, Sundays being their busy day, you know. At least," she said, "her face, the clergyman's wife's, *her* face, sparkled with a little bit of interest when we talked about the novels we were reading."

When she paid her monthly visit home — and this would disconcert Fi — Gillian developed a habit of sitting on the verandah to stare across the hills undulating from the Hindmarsh's. She stared at the trees flourishing to hide the crests of Newrybar's rooftops from the highway. She stared at the trees spreading their canopies over the back of the house to conceal the graduating descent over many kilometers down to the sea. And, in a hushed voice Fi hated for not being like her old one, Gillian said that she had not seen the beauty before. "More like heaven, you know, Fi. We're on top of the world here in a sort of a way, you know." Her smile was quick and shy. Like an old person's sharing a *bon mot*, or a little wisdom with those untried by life.

They had been shrill girls clambering over buttressed roots, Fi and her sister. Gillian pushed a basket into Fi's downstretched hands. Fi lifted the painted basket with a chequered cloth tucked over its contents. Then Gillian, feet and hands securing a hold to hoist the weight of her body up, swung to sit in the crook of a wide, low branch. Once settled, the sisters sat with the basket between them. They giggled and kicked their feet and dramatically retold favourite scenes from storybooks, and they ate the lamingtons and cup-cakes Muriel had prepared for their picnic.

The wind lifted their hair. Smells of sun on grass drifted on the breezes. Sometimes they turned their heads to catch a sniff of seasalt, and they looked through rustling leaves across lush hills rolling from the back of the farm to the Pacific Ocean scudding up the beaches round Byron Bay.

Hills, swathed in vibrant light, were empty of humanity. An early morning dew spackled the air too keenly. Sunshine burst hot all over briar roses. Blueness invaded lime green. Newrybar. It is the purple prose describing the real thing.

Under the clouds and not at all mindful she is already in paradise, Muriel shuffles through the door onto the verandah, tea things clinking when she lowers the tray onto the top step. The reassuring shape of a teapot, a hand-on-hip, hand-in-mid-air, pot-bellied indolence, tips across the story of Fi and Gillian in which the present continues to unravel their past and poke exasperating holes in their future.

Relying on a complacency they easily indulge, one squints at the faraway and swings a leg over the banisters. The older sister, splaying her toes on the wall made of ceiling board, bunching her rumpled skirt up against her crutch and raising one leg to inspect it for scratches and little hairs, frankly admires the smoothness of her skin. They could be single women discussing waxing and other beauty treatments. They are in fact discussing Gillian's thesis, how many more edits she expects to do. When Muriel fusses with a knife, she listens in wonderment to her girls' talk. Indulgently, she drops huge pieces of sponge cake on little floral plates. Gillian winces, and with a groan, exclaims, "Oh, Mum! I'm getting fAAt, you know!"

Sitting on the top step near her tray, Muriel curls her toes under the hem of her skirt and passes her hands under her skirt to hug her ankles. With swelling pride, she listens to her very clever girls. Elbowing the tempo of her girls' erudite discussion, her teacups happily crook their thin handles, but the two women, her adult daughters, turn on her with questions again. "Mum. Can you work the farm?" "Can you afford to hire help?" "Milk the cows?" "Yeees. Why not get rid of the cows and grow some sort of crop?" "Wouldn't that be too labour intensive?"

Offended, Muriel is annoyed to hear herself sounding like a tired old and dependant relative. She grumpily tells them that she had thought about selling and living in the city. "But," and she is genuinely worried, "how'd' I know what the neighbours're like? I mean," and the thought is perplexing, "what if they're wretches I can't get on with?"

Making light of her mother's predicament, Fi flings her hand up in the air. Gillian lets her sister free to confront Muriel with the flip side of the problem. "Mum! Do you think the neighbours who could easily live next to you are born yet?"

Fi is sitting with her back to Muriel. Muriel cannot properly see her younger daughter's face. Pausing in her ritual with teacups, she registers a quiver of uncertainty that she is her daughter's joke. Gillian, watching her mother hesitate, folds her hands over the small mound of her stomach again. She asks Muriel about the farm.

Muriel breathes through the steam rising up from her tea. Her words hesitant, she makes clear her appreciation that the farm, as real estate to be subdivided and sold in parcels, is a valuable asset. But she reveals she is having a tussle with the shire council which, by not responding to the needs anticipated by increased development, were creating future problems that would diminish the quality of the land. Fi, astonished to hear her mother speak with such coherence, asks, "Like what f'r instance?" Muriel snappily grunts. "Problems," she says. "Like the water supply. Sanitation. How the blocks should be serviced. There's no proper planning." Then, as an afterthought, she adds as if to reassure Fi she is the mother she has always known, "Damned men. All of them. Damned stupid men! Know nothing!"

A wave of heat and nausea sucks Gillian's stomach in. She sweats at the temples and, when she suggests Muriel should spend some money doing up the farmhouse — "Make it more comfortable. It could do with a coat of paint. New gutters." — her mouth dries up, muddying her voice. The teapot dips towards her like the rocking horse from a child's story warning her of things to come. Her hand pushes a sweated strand of hair off her face. Her lips burn.

Fi spins off the banisters. She leans against it, toeing the gaps in the floorboards. Underneath there are certain to be dolls' limbs and marbles, ends of crayons and weird messages shrill tree-climbing girls had written to each other. She looks at Gillian. She does not like to ask why her sister is suddenly ashen. She looks at Muriel anticipating with pleasure her future wealth when she sells the hilltops cooled by sea breezes. But her mother and her sister, she believes, are incapable of making pragmatisim their guiding light. They prefer, she notes, to curl inside themselves where they found soft strategies to solve their problems.

Impatient with poorly thought out solutions, Fi turns away from the two of them. Servicing the blocks Muriel dreams she might sell will take years and, snatching the ugly sight of the neighbour's glittering red brick house, Fi rests her eyes on the nothing other than grass and trees and distant hills receding into a purpling haze to meet, and to become, sky. Wherever she looks, she sees the dominant sky.

"Selling the cows?" she asks. She is circumspect about her mother's ability to manage on her own.

"I'll keep a house herd," Muriel mutters in reply, advising that there is a boy nearby. "Studying at high school. He's offered to do the milking. Needs pocket money."

She arches her neck and, drawing her body up with the pointedness of her judgement, she says he has two sisters. "Two sisters," she repeats. "Pretty little girls. And a baby boy. A HALF-brother." Muriel steels to her unswerving belief, "Mother's one of these single mothers. Can't manage without exploiting the kids."

Gillian sinks down into the sofa. Fi follows the sinking down into the kapok and broken springs, and a worst thought stings her brain lucid.

Then Muriel, uncannily and without a hint of a warning, wanders away from her judgemental self into someone else who declares in a happy voice, confiding and laughing softly, that she is going to travel. "Yes! Travel! I've never been further than Sydney to the south and Brisbane to the north." Like an awkward schoolgirl, she paddles in her lap with a crumpled handkerchief when she announces, "I'm going to England! In the springtime! Daphne said we should go together while we still can."

"To visit the queen!" shrieks Fi, and she laughs. Gillian laughs with her, and the sisters swap jokes about Mum and her sister, Daphne, taking tea with Betty Windsor on the chamomile lawn. Muriel, again uncertain she is their joke or their joker, tightens her fist in her lap, but before she grinds fighting words through her teeth, her shoulders slump and something like her will languishes. Under her fixed judgements, her world is unsteady. Muriel is afraid her feet will not find their balance to support her wherever she chooses to go.

Gillian cocks her head at an angle and Fi slouches against the rails, advising sardonically, "Don't forget! Have as many lovers as you like. Just don't marry them. Or we'll lose the farm."

Fi stares meaningfully at Gillian.

Muriel does not see her daughter staring, indeed glaring, at her older sister. Nor does she hear Fi demanding, "Gillian. Are you ...?" Muriel, deeply hurt by Fi, curls her mouth up one cheek, and she packs the tray. With difficulty, she heaves herself up, and she looks across to the treetops shielding the village from view. Breathing heavily through her open mouth, she bends to pick up the tea things. She waddles on painful feet down the hallway to the kitchen where her husband Jim had put in a wall of windows. When she presses her stomach against the bench, her face softens, her memory taking her back to the day he announced his intention to see the sea meeting the sky, shyly adding, "Like t'enjoy m'tea with a view!"

Reminding herself not to become too preoccupied with useless rage against her younger daughter's insensitivities, she puts the tray down, freeing her hand to rub at her eye. Like Gillian, Muriel is afraid of being alone in her old age which, she believes, muttering to herself as she fills the sink with dishwashing liquid, shaking her head and making her mouth into a skewed line, is upon her.

Above the winking lip of a china teacup, Muriel catches a glimpse of a restless glistening she knows is the far distant sea.

The telephone ringing loudly snatches Gillian away from Fi's questioning. Sensitive to the wounds Fi's unkind words inflict on Muriel and too happy with the life inside herself to do anything about it, she suspends caring about Fi's suspicion that she is pregnant. Muriel calling her to the phone pulls her right into the present. She creeps from under Fi's half-finished question. Angered by her family's rational prudishness, the petulant Gillian slaps her bare feet down the hallway to take up the handset. She leaves Fi to float her mood to tangle up in the tree tops.

Fi is mindful of a deep evensong, rustling in quick tempo up to the highest boughs, roars for a moment then descends, rapidly softening where the small leaves hush to lose their murmuring painfully and sadly above the arc of itself. An old tree quavers, asserting an angered man's ancient fear that he has a right to know who he might be fathering, whether he wants to or not, and how it should be done. And something of these desperate pleadings rush with the breeze to lunge down the hallway, supporting Patrick's insistent questioning after Gillian's well-being. "And have you thought of how I feel? Yet?"

"For Christ's sake, Gillian?"

Muriel is suddenly hearing her favourite daughter yelling down the phone, "Patrick! Stop blubbering!" The elderly mother hurries out of the kitchen to stand at the seaside end of the hallway with a tea towel wrapped round a teacup and over her hand. Fi, she sees, is a black shape leaning on the doorjamb at the front entrance to the house.

Light ripples round a concentrated well of awful soundlessness into which Gillian's voice rings clear, "I want this baby, Patrick! I want it very much and if you don't understand that having babies and getting married and setting up some kind of suburban idiocy is not one and the same thing, TOUGH".

Perhaps a strange effect of the distant glistening is running across the back kitchen windows. Perhaps the trees' branches are playing with the setting westerly sun. Later, when they had time to take in the information that Gillian was going to have a baby — that she was going to be a single mother, jeopardising the career she worked so hard to have — neither Fi nor Muriel admit to seeing a woman's lipless face smiling loosely above her widely circling skirt. Neither would talk about it. They had been looking into a light rippling like shallows the sun shone through. Whether the seaside or the front of the house, they were not sure where this fracturing came from.

Occupying all their attention, Gillian is standing on the carpeted floor where they may have seen the creature neither of them will ever admit is a true thing at all. She is beaming at them, daring them to accept or reject her and her baby. But she herself cannot accept that Patrick is struggling with a man-sized fury he cannot contain. She wants to, but she cannot dismiss him. Gillian is unable to freeze out her love of him, but she refuses to consider living with him. Perversely, according to Patrick, she refuses to have a go at finding out if there is enough elbow room for him to live with her and their child. Nothing will discourage her from looking after her baby on her own.

But Gillian cannot tell him she is afraid she is sinking under the wide encircling skirts of a ghostly woman who, visiting her at night, sings a strange lament that washes through a tidal bay. Oppressing her is the fearful thought that she is, by having this child, allowing herself to become somehow bewitched.

With a malevolent strength, her body buoys her up. It is then that she is able to lean towards Fi through the questions and the accusations that she is dilatory. She passes over the doubts harrowing her pleasure in the life quickening inside her to that place where both sisters' girlish eyes, swimming through a tree's branches when a breeze played lightly with their hair, looked at blue and blue and blue.

♓

14. *history*

A prau glides across a lapless sea, its purple mainsail stretched wide, the teal jib upending a square. White circles the head of the dark figure standing in the stern. An oil tanker slices the sea at its back from port to starboard.

Is this a photo image marketing the ageless quality of natural fibres and colours, something pasted up on billboards? A tourist pegs it, a perfect exposure, and vainly tries to remember where she snapped the shot.

Perhaps it is an agelessness opening, time sweeping an instant. Where memory is extending, a history collapses in 1992 under future expectations.

Jacqui Dark is sitting in an unwalled restaurant roofed over a pier. She looks up sweatily from peeling chillied prawns. She sees a prau with purple and teal-blue sails slide across the path of an oil tanker.

The prawns, she will write to Kel, *were delicious*.

At that same moment, Madam Khor Chin-pei looks across the desk at a middle-aged accountant employed by her family's bank in Penang. She is complaining that the facilities in both Lake Toba and in Penang are hopelessly inadequate for her to network her investments effectively. All her transactions, she is saying, should be hooked-up by computer to a satellite. "I should not need to come here! In person," she is declaring, wishing her nephew, Wang Shi-zheng, was still alive to be by her side.

The accountant watches Madame Khor's manicured fingernail flitter over the document in front of her. She is buying a cattle station in Australia. He has advised her not to, and he is hoping she never will learn how to network, send him e-mail, dictate from Lake Toba. Imperiously. Like the tragic dowager she believes she is.

When the oil tanker glides past the E & O and the prau disappears over the horizon towards Sumatra, Badul Mukhapadai is having lunch with Patrick Dreher. In the musty, chilled interior of the City Bayview Hotel, Patrick is asking Badul about the story about the ghost resident in the house on Jalan Dunn where he used to live. "Bit of a fantasy, I suppose," in some way adds credence to the additional information "'T's a used car lot now" that he mumbles almost inaudibly.

Patrick believes he is listening to an Information Resources Manager and a long-time resident of Penang, one involved in the local conservation movement. But Badul veers off the subject of the womanly ghost. He has many contemporary problems on his mind. When blessed with an audience, Mr Mukhapadai expands his opinions about the new technologies with some extravagance. And Patrick's attention wanders to the diminished screen of the television above the bar where a young woman dressed for an earlier decade of this century in sprigged voile is stepping between punters at a racetrack.

Indulging his passion for taking his time over a glass of beer, Badul is invoking his pet thesis. "By these beamings of information from here to there, Mr Dreher, we have a world where even autistic children, famous for their introversion, may be hooked up and conversing. I find this most extraordinary, that the privacy, once the privileged terror of an autistic, should become a part of the public space, when at the same time political freedom to access information, Mr Dreher, is an issue inadequately resolved."

Patrick watches a pretty face under a straw picture hat, and the camera slides back to show she is clutching a cream bag in her cream gloved hand. Badul's voice murmurs under the image, "Politically, the ramifications are not illuminating."

She captivates Patrick's attention, deafens him to "Economics is indeed a dismal science."

Badul delivers his thesis with the clarity of the convicted, his voice rising with his delivery of its most profound point, "That this most grey of sciences most unfortunately visits on all the nations in this region a dismal preoccupation with consumerism, forsaking liberty. True political liberty, Mr Dreher, is a privilege too many have not ever experienced. At bottom, ordinary amenities, considered usual by you, are not available to the vast and most benighted majority. The Gopis and the Sasras are still without running water to their houses. In the meantime, others fly to London regularly for the theatre."

Patrick, engrossed by the pretty woman, the one who is altogether more striking to look at than the other women in the grandstand, looks at the women looking at the horses as they are being led to their cages. Badul, shaking his head sadly, persists, "Let me tell you, this networking, this sharing of great dialogues, this freedom to discourse by satellite is illusory, my dear Mr Dreher."

Patrick nods, as people do when they are poor audience to an uncertainly passionate speech. He is too amazed by the man in the frame of the tee vee. Dressed in creams and a Panama, he touts for the women's bets, turning, his head filling the square. And the man tips his hat back onto his crown, smiling as if he is possessed of a superior and secret knowledge that he may, under mellowing conditions, be prepared to share. Badul, sipping beer, raises his voice to expound, "The sheer abundance of data produces such an elaboration of cross-referencing the systems break down. Too slow, the keywords must be too specific." When he says, "Alternatively, the cross-referencing becomes broad, neutralised, useless for researchers, serious scholars," a pair of male lips mouths words.

A bottle looms, it fills the screen. Expanding his thinness to fit with his exposition, Badul says, "There are too many obstructions to accessing the basic data, too many political interferences, and I am telling you this is no triangle of economic growth but the vassal state of business." And droplets of refreshing coldness overtake the square screen as if this evocation of history — a past empire languishing at the racetrack — is signified by a woman's pretty head followed by the chill condensing off a bottle of Guinness.

At last looking away from the advertisement, Patrick agrees, "Change is rapid."

Startled by Patrick's bland face, Badul has a sudden fear for his daughter.

Fish see it all. In scales like lenses on the underside of their bellies.

Fish see a shadow cross another.

If the same prau glides in front of the same oil tanker offshore Batam, an Indonesian island near Singapore where Fi Hindmarsh may be attending an investors' conference, her sister, Gillian, may be peeling peaches at Newrybar, Australia, where she calls, "Lee…igh!!… Leeeee…igh! … Leigh?"

Can that be right?

Surely, in 1992, Gillian is in Sydney, calling to Leigh as she goes out the front door of her small house to her evening classes or meetings at any one of the city's universities, instructing the child carer where to find the cat food and what time she should microwave the frozen quiche for Leigh's dinner. Leigh, is he nine? Or ten? Does it matter? For him, one year flows into another, whether he swings through the branches of a favourite tree in bucolic Newrybar, or explores the possibilities of the latest game on his VCR in Sydney, that harbour blue city.

Gillian will settle into a kind of umbrage. In a few years' time, at the turn of the twentieth century into the twenty-first, she will be that classic Australian woman deceived by a promised thrill in life. By squeezing her eyes shut, she has acquired an ability to look past her disgust in both the hostile and the bland to the small change she has accumulated to establish a comfortable place for her son and herself.

Will she regret her lack of liaisons, her refusal to court the dangers of following her body's desire for men like Badul Mukhapadai? Does she allow fantasy to steer her course through her mapped world?

If, at the nervous centre of her mouth where she presses the cap of a fountain pen, she deliberates on how to present her credentials to a selection committee for a promotion, or how to complete an application for a grant to fund her further research, she will harbour no such regret or give any fantastic speculation a thought.

A delicacy about Gillian, some would say 'a sense of integrity', used to prohibit her from manoeuvring herself onto the selection committees to secure the selection of herself. Her possession, after her mother died, of a beautiful farm in partnership with her sister has not diminished in her a sense of deprivation and neurotic guilt. Over the years, a little fear has seeped through to make her, Gillian Hindmarsh, PhD, Sydney, wise to the world. She cannot endure being sidelined. The bitter memory of teaching in a primary school on the dusty western plains where she suffered community indifference whipped a chill wind through her heart. Love and honour and fair play had no place, she learned, when survival was at stake. Not thinking twice, she will subvert goodness and brightly nominate the one who will agree to nominate her, believing she is, after all, worthy of the recognition she seeks.

On the other hand, if in her future days, Gillian slices peaches and listens to the breezes murmuring through Newrybar's tree tops, she may indulge all the time in the world to snare herself in regrets. Prideful motherhood, she may discover, is a circumstance that intersects personal ambitions.

Doubtlessly, Gillian will wrestle life. For becoming a woman possessed of an inner turbulence fractured by a punishing will is not on her agenda. Patrick or someone else may very well circle his arm round her waist, whispering, "Nice'n slow, let's do it." And she may just do that, although, notwithstanding pleasure, she will be endlessly fascinated and exhausted by having to manage the mothering-with-teaching-and-research performance, the two career juggling act.

Mostly, Leigh says he does not hear when his mother calls.

Fish see, and they flick their tails when they hear some. A fungus spreading over their skin blurs the outlines of formless rocks, a pier's struts. Brown weeds waver above a dreamt world in which a future Leigh will linger in rumpled sheets, watching the light playing across the naked body of a young woman. In this future they see him playing in, he is touching her hair, his fingers rubbing together strands of something like fine rain. Surprised, he may touch her shoulder, and run his hand over her buttocks, and he will caress a velvetiness he had not thought possible of skin. Lazily, he smells sex and he wants more, and he rubs his chest and moves his legs.

In this magic moment, the room is anywhere, he will be anywhere, she is anyone, they will be holidaying exclusively at a nameless resort on a nameless island that looks like everywhere pictured in the travel brochures. Perhaps this one is the Mutiara at Penang, a white pleasure city surrounded by a landscaped paradise scored into the escarpment at Batu Ferringhi. It could be, and it could be anywhere else tropical, her father paying for the drinks and, outside, a vast ocean sighing for a sunset.

Leigh chucks a grin and his future self slithers into the humidity under the sheets. His sudden movement wakes the young woman. She grumbles and tugs at the sheets he drags over himself, and she giggles and he tugs at the sheets and she giggles some more and he rolls on top of her. In the space of a withheld shriek, she passes her hand over his cheek and roughs up his hair. "Okay!" she says. "You will be my Australian boy."

Leigh has a sudden thought she might not recall his name when she talks about her 'Australian boy' over a drink in a hometown cafe. He eyes her steadily, and he says, knowing his desire is to forget who she is, "Okay. I don't mind *you* remembering *me*."

His famous crinkle-cheeked smile winks his left eye.

After a sprung silence, the sheets billow over a crazily buckling mattress.

Fish backs flash, fish tails whip.

They know a woman's ghost no longer glides at the evening tide on the leeside of Penang Island. They know a funny little light will brighten Leigh's eye. They wait, these fishes, waiting for Leigh to sink into another place, gathering his strength for the future they predicted will belong to the lipless one. The ghost's future. She will live with him, Leigh. And, like his namesake of another race and another time in history, Li'tsieng, Leigh will cause the fishes consternation by spending a lot of time with many women who they know are not right for him.

In someone else's life, a womanly smile widens over a spoonful of rice, and Badul Mukhapadai may, for a moment, feel transformed into a godlike being. For inside his head, his reality dips, her smile lopsides and she shares with him her knowledge about the conservation of Penang's old buildings, new technologies and old literatures. Badul spins through his dream of her, her hair ripping away from her skull, clothes billowing around her. She transports him back to the poetry of his youth when he longed for a highly perfumed romance among flowers with the *sarod* strumming *ragas* from stoney recesses to a woman, any woman. In his daily life, she was, for a time, Mei-mei, his wife. In his dreams there were many, some named and some unnamed. One was Gillian Hindmarsh. At the turn of the century, he is startled to see this woman alive in his daughter, Savitri.

Savitri Mukhapadai.

An impossibly Malaysian Chinese Brahmin, she is a strange, mixed race kind of *çandi* yet to slip from her father's fussy protection.

She may act as a solicitor for one of the Wang Penang interests, wrongly stepping into another kind of fishy tryst with a member of that family. Savitri is most unlike the Rose of 1941. Not needing a love affair to discover qualities redeeming her an identity, her story will not make a claim on fiction screened cinematically. Scenes from her life may find their way into travel, banking or perfume ads beamed into living rooms. She may be the subject of biographical articles written to inspire young women to pursue an education that focuses on the professions, rather than concentrate one's energy on the kind of glamour that leads to housekeeping. And, being coolly sophisticated, Savitri will not act impulsively when she observes bodies react in sometimes alarming ways.

If Savitri should find Leigh Dreher in some unlikely place, she may pause to see through a sudden sexual zinging the swagger and the famous crinkle-cheeked smile. Fabling Sinbad's love for adventure in her own life and perhaps challenging her body's pain, she may 'weigh up the odds' and have fun with a 'toy boy'. And she may find herself embracing a long history of passion with heartache, giving herself a hard time by being difficult, forcing Leigh into uncharacteristic protestations of love accompanied by some extravagant gestures, thus completing an unfinished affair of the past by satisfying both their present fleshy states of being.

If she does meet Leigh and they do not have an affair, a hideous ghost will heave with the sea's currents through Savitri's dreamings. That story told with sound effects and no conversation on the big screen at the cinema could be poignant. With sentimental fanfare and a lot of twittering, the same could be an instruction warning girls to be on the lookout for love least they should become unhappily forgotten.

All the same, the fish will writhe where the bottoms of harbours are soft with heavy metal pollution. Swimming forever and under a prau with purple and teal-blue sails sliding in front of an oil tanker, they watch for these moments they predicted. They understand this golden woman with liquid black eyes is the blonde one of the 40s. They know she is the reincarnation of the womanly ghost who keened a lament for her lost lover in the late evenings of December, frightening the fishermen with her ghastly smile — until, in 1982, dredging for a bridge's struts thrust her into life.

♓

15. *underlying the universe*

Anyway, who is this woman, this Rose swimming through dreams? Where does she come from?

If there were a single unifying law underlying the universe, where would she figure?

A crimson dorsal fin, elaborately feathered, wavered above a small fish body. Its eyes wide open, it sleeps beside reeds in a tropical sea, waiting for Rose to sink into its domain, but where was she, if she is the sum total of her memories?

In London, 1927, kicking her heels against chintz covers as if she was an equestrian, Rose's memories began with a trick she had of leaving her six year old body under her Nanny's milky blue eye, leaving her fingers running up and down piano keys, leaving Eeyore and Piglet and Winnie the Pooh's wishes on pages she splotched with paint. In her head, she galloped over seas through wind and rain from cold to hot until she reined in at being three years old where the smells were both familiar and arresting.

There she took the hand of an old Chinese man whose stick-thin bow legs hurried him up a red pebbled driveway. His toothless smile made her heart beat fast. With renewed zest, she skipped ahead of him, her nose snaffling up smells of hot sesame oil and garlic and ginger and star anise, chicken and pork fat, kerosene cooking fuel and the rich sweet stench of overripe durian.

The *amah* smiled and gave her sweets and told her stories about the spirits dwelling at the bottom of the garden where *pomelo* trees grew. She told her stories of horses flying through the night to strange lands. They carried princesses on their backs, sometimes with a sailor called Sinbad who rescued them from ogres. Sometimes the horses carried their precious cargo to their kingly fathers' castles where all children were safe with their regal mothers.

Rose looked to see where the old man was. She spied him staggering under the weight of a rocking horse. He set it down beside her bed. It had glass eyes. With great solemnity, she put its eyes under her pillow to stop it from going anywhere.

This little Rose was a heart squeezed down by a bleakly expensive hearth. She was born on Penang Island. When she was three, she was sent back to England, set to steam from port to port with a brood of little children who, like herself, were catatonic with the fear of abandonment.

The ship's crew were experienced carers of colonial children sent back to 'the home country' to grow straight and healthy. They staged puppet theatres and pantomimes and showed comic silent movies. Organised games, parties attended by clowns, visitations from the characters out of La Fontaine's fairy tales failed to shake these children out of their lethargy. At night, they shrieked in their sleep. They woke to find their pillows soggy with tears and their stomachs knotted up in awful tight balls.

And she was by far the youngest. It was more usual to send seven year olds back to relatives and schools instilling in them the pride of being British. Rose, her aunts took great care to tell her, was mothered by a woman who could not be bothered with little girls.

The perpetual rites of tea interfered with her flights by horseback, but Rose was skilled at staying firmly fixed in her fantasies. She gave the horse its eyes, swung into its saddle to gallop to a place where she might discover if long forgotten arms had wound round her little body — if a careful hand had pulled a brush through her hair, if her mother had told her stories, if her mother had sung her lullabies and taught her little wisdoms about clean handkerchiefs, neat socks and wide, pink sashes ... But the pictures never changed. An old Chinese man always struggled up a red-pebbled driveway. A wide-faced *amah* told stories in a pungent and noisy kitchen. A horse rocked across the breadth of sky. The pictures, like the ones in her picture book about a sailor called Sinbad, flickered and careened as if a sheet wavered unsteadily on the deck of a ship rolling at sea. And the Rose who Rose longed to be took out the eyes of her phantom horse to stop it flying off without her.

The breadth of oceans and the magical moon.

Rose's grandmother played endless games of bridge. Her grandfather spent late nights at the Club. Her aunts pointed their chins and uttered shrill judgements. Her uncles clapped their hands above their buttocks and rocked on their heels. And Rose never met the regal mother whose arms might have encircled her a long time ago. Rose's mother never made the voyage from Penang to London to see her daughter.

Fish upended a story and sucked at it with their fleshy lips. They digested the news that Rose's mother had run off with her favourite dancing partner, "AUSTRAYlian! Would you believe?" With a lace handkerchief held to her cheek, Rose's grandmother said she believed he owned a lot of land. "Quite a lot. Horse breeding. And sheep," she added with a weepy squeak. The aunts, hoping to improve matters for the child, told Rose she had a little sister called Lydia who lived 'in the outback'. But, disturbed by their sister's disregard for her duties as a mother and a wife, the aunts and the grandmother did not notice the girl in their charge was in some sort of distress.

Her father sent her birthday and Christmas cards. He wrote no letters. Her mother sent her nothing. Rose was passed round her circle of relatives. If one had the wit to ask her to 'bear up, now', she would have sat up, shocked, trying to register a series of bright images of people and faces and tables and chairs and curtains and things. Then she would have crumpled in a heap again, nursing a pain rather than remembering anything special.

Her cousins complained she was dopey. She did not make firm friends at the schools her uncles sent her to. One or two teachers noticed that she was unusually withdrawn, but her aunts failed to notice. As far as they were concerned, she was one of those quiet girls found dressed in jodhpurs brushing down horse coats. They were not the sort of women who hung around to hear the girl whispering in horse ears the letters she wanted her father to write. Drifting unremarked from day's end to day's end, from year to year, Rose looked ordinarily ordinary.

But a hard truth locked across her throat. Words, unreleased, slid down her gullet in big lumpy sobs. In her head, Rose killed her mother. Buried her. Under a mud slide.

Her aunts discussed the awful mess she made, biting her fingernails to the quick.

She may have fallen asleep at the stables, she may have slumped on a sofa in a sunroom, she may have simply gone to bed one night, her mood especially sullen. Whatever may have been the circumstances, Rose was surprised if not elated when, next to her bed stood a horse. She saw its long slow rock. Its glass eyes popped out of their sockets. As if time stretched, the eyes traced an unhurried trajectory, but she did not see them land anywhere. She climbed out of bed and clung to the horse's neck, whispering for it to fly through the air. Its throat bulged. Its legs could not release themselves from its rockers to beat at its eyes which were suddenly lumps sticking in its throat. In vain, the horse thrashed. The night, too cold for her ropey body, froze. She slipped off the horse's back into a bed of letters her father never wrote.

Nanny made tea and a soup the colour and consistency of dishwater. Rose lay still. Her aunts and uncles crowded round her. They exhorted her to get up. Horrified by all this hitherto ungiven attention, she kept her mouth shut. A light breeze ruffled the bed linen. The window was open. The curtains billowed then pleated coyly. Snowflakes fluttered in. Rose shivered. She was purpley blue from cold, but Nanny instructed her aunts and uncles fresh air was right for her. And she pinched Rose's nose. She forced Rose's mouth open. She ladled the soup over the edge of Rose's teeth. Then Nanny cried out, alarmed by two glass eyes that peered at her from the girl's throat.

The aunts and uncles ordered Nanny to stick her fingers down Rose's throat and hook the eyes out. They frowned and shouted and wagged their fingers. They said they were obliged to put Rose up, provide for her and set her right. They clutched the bedstead, and they frostily demanded Rose's unreserved gratitude. And she pulled the bedsheets up under her chin, and ran her hand under them to touch her breasts and the rough patch of hair growing where her legs met. She panicked when she discovered she was suddenly naked. But she did not cry out. She lay on her side and tried to smile, hoping that if she looked happy they would all go away.

The aunts formed a circle. With sisterly concern for each other, they turned their backs on their niece and shared their condemnations of this dependant sent to them by an errant sister-in-law. The uncles did funny things with their lips, pocketed their hands and stuck out their stomachs. They were heard tsk-tsking when the horse rocked up. Rose opened her mouth to greet it. The eyes flew out of her throat across the room, knocking Nanny flat. The terrified aunts shrieked, and the officious if not fastidious uncles caused pandemonium.

Rose leaped onto the horse's back. It rocked off. Naked, she rocked by horseback to a hot place full of spicy smells where she hoped her father stood like a king in his dancing suit, puzzling over a hazy thought that he might have a daughter somewhere. Wrapping herself in his unwritten letters, Rose called out, "Daddy!" But she could not put a face to the fatherly figure dressed for dancing. And her throat tightened at the loss of her father dancing under a tropical moon, and her face went blue at the thought of her mother choking under mud on a cattle station somewhere in Australia. Dejected, she let the letters drop, let thousands of sheets of paper float. If she had a father, she believed he would look straight through her to the other thought of the wife who troubled him.

The horse neighed. It kicked crazed heels high. She smelt its sweat. She tossed and twisted but she could not slide off its back. She could not escape melting her body into an inner space. Ears and eyes, throat and lips vanished into her naked centre. Transparent, she expired, sort of died.

The horse bucked and raged. It sped through frost. Spittle from its mouth hung in icicles. Foam frothing round its bit froze and, kicking higher, smashing smashing smashing a nightspace, the horse woke Rose up to a dream about walking barefooted over glass which lay half-buried under a thick muddy ooze.

Fish eyes, always open, saw all this in a globule of moonlight dropped to the ocean floor.

Days swayed in and time dripped down a wall. Flickering into emerging future moments, the present promised repeats.

When she was sent back to Georgetown, Penang, where her uncle, Cedric, lived, her Willoughby aunts and uncles hoped Rose might 'do the right thing', unburden them of her, go husband-hunting. Out there. In the Far East.

Correctly, they counted on Cedric's wife, Rose's Aunt Margaret. She 'did the right thing'. They knew she would. At the de-luxe hotels, the E & O and the Runnymede, she chaperoned Rose who spent the nights dancing with a lot of eligible young men who came East to 'make good'. Rose smiled at a swelling procession of Russians and Viennese Jews, Armenians and Serbs, and other people preoccupied with escaping history.

Then a young man from one of those Straits Chinese families negotiated a way around the social inequities of the colonial good-time island. The Willoughbys had not bargained on that and, at the time, they did not know about it. They only heard a whisper about it after the Frightful Years of the Second World War. "Fortunate," they opined, "that things turned out the way they did. I mean to say." A cough bumped with a belling *ping!* against those few crystal sherry glasses that survived the bombing.

Was it just as well things turned out the way they did? What would the Willoughbys have done if Rose and Li-tsieng ... What would the Wangs have done if ... It has to be said that consternation would have afflicted both Wangs and Willoughbys. In this instance, the war was most convenient, sparing the aunts and uncles of both families confrontation with the simple truth that Li-tsieng's caresses awakened in Rose's naked body a quality of calm such she had never before known.

The fish, however, understood Rose had no spoken words for how she felt. In her skin, she retreated to a stillness where a secret, rocking on a horse's back, waited for the insight of her eyes. Unclouded by longing and fear, she touched emptiness. She sank into the belly of herself, and gathered her energies. Rose let her illusory self float past the pleasured moment where she knocked against serenity.

S adly, history laid its claim on Rose and Li-tsieng.

On December 11, 1941, the streets of Georgetown filled with a mass of upturned faces, mesmerised by shards of blackening red spitting through daylight. An amazed crowd watched Japanese aircraft dart down, then swoop upwards. The sky filled with dramatic orange blasts split with pinks and smothered by yellows. People jostled for a better view, trying to understand what it was they were looking at. And the Japanese gunners, thrilled to drive hard above the crowd-filled streets, aimed their machine guns and murdered the spectators of war.

Li-tsieng sat under the sea that day, at a long dining table. He sat in his family's submarine dining hall, picking fish bones from between his teeth. Rose lay on a red satin sofa, her fingers curling loosely above her forehead. He asked, "Why are you here? Why haven't you sailed with the other women and children?"

A drifting crab struck out a feeble claw. It scraped glass.

Rose stirred. She turned to face the watery green walls of the room before she rolled over and sat up, and she said, without any hint of emotion, "They left me. They were packing and I thought they were packing for me too. I packed for me. Then I heard you were back from Chile. I suppose I should've said where I was going, I mean I did dash off rather without explaining. Well, it seems when I was with you, they left. Shipped out. West Australian Service, I discovered, I must suppose they are now safely in Perth. No note. Nothing. Just an empty house. They were supposed to go to Colombo. Spectacular bad timing on my part, Li-tsieng, letting them slip off like that."

Li-tsieng glanced at her often as she spoke. He ate deliberately and with pleasure, but he was distracted by the way the material of her dress rustled over her stomach and hips when she stood up.

Rose slowly slid over to the gramophone and flipped through a collection of records. She slipped one out of its envelope. Her slender neck arched, the light exposing its sinuous fragility. Li-tsieng stopped picking at fish flesh when she dropped the record onto the turntable and gently let the needle arm down. He raised his napkin to his lips, and stood up.

Without hesitation, they walked into each other's arms. To the strains of Al Bowlly crooning for an enchanting smile to make the whole world right, they danced round the submarine room, brushed passed the velvet drapes closing over the entrance to ante-rooms, and swept away from the greenly glass walls where light rippled and fish eyes popped. Her hair, as always, surprised him. Loving its silkiness, he rested his cheek against her head, and he heard her quiet voice explain, "I'm a bad girl, you see, Li-tsieng. You have made me a bad girl. I lowered British esteem. My affair with you affronts the Empire's prestige. And this is my punishment. To dance with you under the sea."

Waiting ...

Waiting ...

Waiting for ...

His fingers pressed her skin more firmly.

On Swettenham Pier, under a briefly calm sky on this fateful December day in 1941, a ship bumped the woods and splintered some, punctuating the end of happier noises humming through the formerly peaceful days of Penang Island. Adults bit their lips and bloodied their mouths, fearfully clinging to their children. White faces, at the edge of a sweltering terror, bowed over baggage when an insect mechanically whirred above their heads.

Close to the ocean floor in the unremitting dark, a hideous fish witnessed a shifting of pressures sounding against a fistule the size of a halogen lamp encumbering its outsized head. From the watery deep, its bulbous eyes sighted Li-tsieng dancing with Rose in a house built like a castle with gardens stretching to the sea. Two rose coloured Greek statues flanked the black marble staircase leading to its porticoed entrance. Staircases led upwards into towered rooms. Walls were panelled with *bois-de-rose* brocade. When the bombs pounded the grounds and the windows burst, cream lace curtains tore inwards, across beds shaped like shells beneath ceilings patterned with lily-of-the-valley and forget-me-nots, innocent of war and Japanese midgets.

The servants screamed and ran up and down stairs, crying for the young master. They looked for him in the bedroom, expecting to find him in the shell-shaped bed with Rose, his paramour, that white woman who brought him the bad luck of an overweening love for an earthly creature. They looked for him in the dressingroom where he may have been brushing down his morning suit, adjusting a pale yellow rose to his button hole before taking up his cane and his top hat, preparing to meet the dreadful woman. They looked for him in the bathroom, hoping they would not surprise him standing naked on the rose-coloured tiles beside the rose-coloured bathtub, a rose-coloured towel draped round his hips.

The servants ran down polished wooden stairs to the dining hall, the strains of Lew Stone's band backing Al Bowlly swinging up to them. And, at the moment the lovers circled the long dining hall, the crooner fell victim to a bomb blitzing London's blackened streets. The lovers clasped their hands between their chests. They pressed their foreheads together. They swayed slightly.

Fear of imminent death speeded up piscine swimming. Fish fins stiffened with resolve, their shocked belief compounding the fear that nature had indeed deserted them. They did not hear him say to her, "Rose! I'm glad I came back." They did not hear her say, "Aah yes, Li-tsieng! It's better that it's come to this!"

When the music stopped, no longer playing for the leisurely dance, the record crackled under the needle, wobbled round and round and round the central pin into an hiatus of silence.

Who, or what were they waiting for?

Eternity?

Love? In perpetuity?

Or a silent moment before the inevitable, the thing they knew would happen?

The hideous fish on the ocean floor dropped its weird head when a bomb slid and hooshed, plunging through bubbling soundlessness. Light irradiated a boiling column, and the glass walls cracked. Water swelled and roared, crushing the room.

She rolled across the satin sofa. It pillowed her broken neck. Her body heaved. A plume of water thrust her up, and she twisted and rolled and bumped against a glaring grey day.

The pieces of Li-tsieng's body were scattered wide. His unidentifiable face floated towards the shore looking for its legs and arms, finding instead ants that scurried through the craters where his brain and eyes should have been. A turgid heat simmered gore. His lost soul flopped into a corner. It shuddered under the inauspicious images of his promised future life.

Agonised by sudden aloneness, Rose sank backwards to reclaim a moment, stepping through unnatural currents to the jagged walls of the glass dining hall. Her dress crinkled and pleated round her hips, her loose head swayed, her hands clasped and unclasped, and her throat, hollowed from the madness of loving too much, tried to cry out, "Come back! ... Come home! ... Come back!" But the words stayed stuck.

The fish whipped heads and tails in consternation. Holding her head steady, they nibbled her lips and kissed her earlobes and nuzzled her eyelids. Her arms wavered, elongating bluishly under the water. The fish raised her up, and carried her up to break the surface with a splashing. The young woman embraced her future the fishes predicted was hers.

Fish backs flash and she grimaces at the evening's pink vapours, yet another and another and another long lapse in time casting her up on the leeside of Penang Island. Suspended on a thread of surprised disbelief that her life should have snapped short so rudely, her spirit lists among detritus with little fishes. Sometimes she is caged behind splayed mangrove roots, sometimes she sweeps over branches dipping into a gently lapping tide, sometimes she hits against rocks concealed under a fresh water stream spilling into a low ebb.

This is Rose, a lipless ghost. For decades, she rolls, pitches, lurches. And in the month of December when palm trees bend over sand to offer their hearts to the moon, a sound like a saxophone horns across a breeze, drawing with it a singing sigh. Some say it is a plaint. Others believe it is the sound of Li-Tsieng's bones searching for their dust and grit, their splintered particles. The wiser women of the fishing villages understand Rose keens to sing him whole again.

And the fish?

Their eyes rotate, gills twitch, scales catch sight of a sighing on breezes. They have heard the stories, they know the bottom line. They are wise when, rippling across the concentricities of time, the music swells for a lover to swim through the learned performance to a pleasure beyond suffering.

A ghost has rolled. A ghost is yearning. Lovers' lips will smile.

And fish are slicing through tides.

Finis

Acknowledgements

While many incidents have been drawn from historical accounts, none of the characters in *fish lips* are historical figures, as this novel is a fiction, a work in which the imagination travels through the decades from 1940 to the year 2000.

I could not have researched the historical material for *fish lips* without libraries and libraians.

Firstly, thanks are due to the librarians of the State Library of New South Wales, especially the Dickson collections; The National Library of Australia, especially the archival resources; Fisher Library, University of Sydney; the National Library of Singapore, most especially for the bound copies of *British Malaya*; and The Library, National University Singapore for its considerable newspaper collections on microfiche.

Secondly, there were books. Mrs Yeap Joo Kim's biography, *The Patriarch* ([Times; n.d.]) and her novel, *of comb, powder & rouge* (Lee Teng Lay; 1992) were usefully evocative and rich in detail. *Memories of a Nyonya* by Queenie Chang (Eastern Universities Press, 1981), a family history that described a mansion of Penang featuring a submarine dining hall. For angles on history, I found an essay *on the railway station* in *A Philosophy Of History: In Fragments* by Agnes Heller inspirational. I should also include *National Revolution in North Sumatra* by Dr Michael van Langenberg, for I used my husband's unpublished PhD thesis for chapter 9, *a nib for a shoe*.

And may I especially thank Mrs Cheah Ai Lin and her husband, Cheah B. K, Emeritus Professor of History (USM, Penang, Malaysia) whose enthusiastic and generous advices encouraged me to continue writing; Sophie Dove and Angela Lowe of the School of Biological Sciences, University of Sydney, for those conversations which circled around fish; to Tim Yap Fun, a gem of a librarian; and Mariapan Karupian and Sergeant Brendan David, both of the Penang Turf Club, for a wonderful morning of significant chatting about the history of horse racing in Penang.

The quotation from Sandy Flitterman-Lewis on page vi was used with permission.

♓